Then Came You

The McPhee Clan

Jillian Hart

Copyright © 2013 by Jill Strickler
All rights reserved.
http://jillianhart.net

Cover Design by Kim Killion, Hot Damn Designs
http://hotdamndesigns.com

E-book Formatted by Jessica Lewis, Authors' Life Saver
http://authorslifesaver.com

Editing by Jena O'Connor, Practical Proofing
http://practicalproofing.com

This is a work of fiction. Names, characters, places, brands, media, and incidents are either the product of the author's imagination or are used fictitiously. The author acknowledges the trademarked status and trademark owners of various products referenced in this work of fiction, which have been used without permission. The publication/use of these trademarks is not authorized, associated with, or sponsored by the trademark owners.

ISBN: 1494232308
ISBN-13: 978-1494232306

CHAPTER ONE

**Bluebell, Montana Territory
Spring 1876**

Oh, no, there he is. Maebry O'Riley skidded to a stop on the boardwalk and peered through the front display window of Gunderson's Mercantile. Through the sun-glazed glass she could plainly see her nemesis, Lawrence Latimer, standing at the front counter, hat in hand, waxing on about something to poor Gemma Gunderson. Maebry's stomach cringed with sympathy as she squinted, bringing the spinster's face into clear focus. Yep, that was the exact look of agony Lawrence Latimer brought out in a woman.

Maebry grimaced. If she set foot inside the store right now, then she would be his next victim. Totally tempting to run in the other direction. She clutched her shopping list in one hand, debating the merits of going back to her employer empty-handed, without the special tea Maureen desired—no, *demanded*. But, that wouldn't be good. Not at all. So that meant running was not an option.

That meant her only option was to face the man. Maebry glanced down at the list she was inadvertently crushing in her palm. Oops. Just went to show how much she didn't want to deal with Lawrence. Frowning, she straightened the paper, palms a little damp, wondering if perhaps hiding was a better solution. Maybe she could duck behind the wagon and wait until Lawrence had finished tormenting Gemma, left the store and gone on his merry way. *Then* it would be safe to go shopping for Maureen's tea.

"I see that." A friendly baritone rumbled behind her, boots clomping to a stop on the boardwalk. "I know what you're thinking."

"Oops, I guess you caught me." She grimaced. She knew that voice, and knew it well. She spun around, squinting in the sunshine at the tall, brawny man with the sun to his back. Golden light outlined the jaunty tilt of his Stetson, the rock-jaw and iron shoulders. She'd know that silhouette anywhere. She squinted up at him. "Gil Blackburn. What are you doing in town?"

"Getting extra feed across the way." The new assistant foreman at the Rocking M Ranch jerked his head toward the store on the other side of the street. "Beckett says he feels a storm on the way. This time of year, and judging by the black clouds to the northwest, it's likely to be a mean one."

"Spring blizzards. Yay. My favorite." She rolled her eyes, wishing she could stop grinning so much. The man just had that effect on her. "Say, I have an idea."

"Uh oh. Women and their ideas scare me." The brawny cowboy's chiseled face softened into a grin.

Straight, white teeth, amazing smile, little glints of mischief in those navy blue eyes. If she let herself, she could be easily dazzled by the likes of Gil Blackburn. Good thing she had no intention of letting herself. She set her chin, determined to ignore his magnificence. She'd managed to do it for the past few months since Gil had hired on at the Rocking M Ranch. That was the way it had to continue to be.

"Oh, then this idea will definitely scare you," she informed him airily, offering him her arm. "I find myself in need of a beau."

"A beau?" He adjusted his hat, a hint of a grin curving his chiseled mouth. "I didn't know. I'm not sure I approve of such a forward woman. I like ladies who know how to let the man make the first move."

"You know perfectly well what I meant. I can read it in your eyes." Those big, gorgeous blue eyes that seemed to say everything about the man. His honor. His character. His kindness. Her heart gave a little leap, hoping her crush on him didn't show. After all, they worked together and, more importantly, she was not a free woman. "Keep in mind that if you don't help me out, I'll make sure every meal you get this week will be cold and burned."

THEN CAME YOU

"Well, little lady, you leave me no choice." He shrugged his impressive shoulders, flashed his dazzling grin. The sunshine bronzed him, warmed his dark brown hair to a chocolate color, outlined him with gold. "You know how I hate cold and burned food."

"I do." She glanced sideways at him, enamored. Why did the man always enamor her? "You're too easy, Gil."

"You mean gullible?"

"That, too."

"If only you didn't cook my every meal, I'd be heading across the street right now ordering oats instead of rescuing you from Lawrence." He reached for the door, gallant as always. "Do you want me to act enamored, or will escorting you through the store be enough?"

"Shh." She elbowed him lightly in the ribs, aware of the solid feel of him. Very solid, very manly. Whew, she felt just a tad dizzy and no surprise that was, as Gil likely rendered any woman he came across light-headed. The saving grace was that he didn't know he was devastatingly handsome. No, Gil was as humble and as down-to-earth as a man could get. Which only made him more attractive, of course.

And made the teensy-weensy, little, miniscule crush she had on him a tad bigger.

The bell above the door jangled merrily, announcing their presence. Both Lawrence and Gemma turned toward the door, Lawrence smiling benevolently beneath his handlebar mustache, Gemma pleading with a *help me* look.

Maebry held up her list, hoping she looked in dire need of assistance. What else could she do, since she'd been in Gemma's shoes more times than she could count, enduring Lawrence's ardent attempts at courting? Girls had to stick together when it came to over-eager bachelors.

"Hi Gemma, I'm afraid I need some help. I have quite a few questions." She strolled into the shop, aware of the strapping man at her side. How could she not be aware of him? "Sorry to interrupt, I see you're with another customer, but you know Maureen."

"That I do." Beaming gratitude, Gemma launched out from behind the counter, her sensible brown dress snapping around her ankles, her practical black shoes drumming a light beat on the wood floor. "Sorry, Lawrence, I have customers. Lovely chatting with you."

"And with you, my fair lady." Lawrence tipped his bowler hat, his rapturous gaze following Gemma's progress away from the counter.

Then his gaze landed on Maebry and turned euphoric.

"Oh, Miss O'Riley." He bowed deeply, as if ready to start a new campaign to win her heart. "What a pleasure. Will I be seeing you at the Montgomery's May Day party tomorrow?"

"Likely, as Maureen has volunteered me as kitchen help for the day." She sidestepped a few inches closer to Gil, hoping Lawrence would get the hint. "So I'll be working."

"Such a pity." Lawrence schooled his too narrow face into an overly sincere show of commiseration. "Maureen should grant you at least part of the day for frivolity. I could save you a dance?"

"Oh, I'm not sure Gil would like that." Really, what did it take for Lawrence to give up? She patted Gil's muscled arm, trying not to notice how strong and manly he was. That was like not noticing the way gravity held your feet to the floor. Her heart gave a little wistful sigh of dreaminess, which she did her best to ignore. "Would you, Gil?"

"No, I'm afraid I wouldn't." Gil planted his feet, all six plus feet of towering muscle and might. "You're not trying to move in on my girl, are you, Latimer?"

"Uh." Lawrence swallowed, his narrow gaze arrowing to the tough, strapping cowboy. "I didn't realize you two were together. I simply assumed you were escorting her to town for ranch business."

"We work together, it's true." A muscle ticked along Gil's strong, square jaw. "But Maebry is my lady now."

"Oh, then congratulations are in order." Lawrence paled, looking disappointed. "You've got a fine one there, the prettiest in the county. Guess I'll be getting on with the rest of my errands. Have a good afternoon, Gemma. I'll see you soon."

"Lovely," Gemma called out a touch sarcastically from somewhere in the aisles of shelving.

Wow, he really was leaving. Just like that. It was really too good to be true. Maebry held her breath as Lawrence left with a jingle of the bell above the door and paraded down the boardwalk out of sight. He was gone. And she hadn't spent thirty minutes or more politely trying to get out of a conversation with him.

"I'm exhausted." Gemma called out from somewhere close, lost behind the tall shelves of goods. "Thank goodness you came along when you did. Maebry, that was excellent, bringing Gil. I've been trying to get rid of Lawrence for the last forty-five minutes."

THEN CAME YOU

"Maybe you need a pretend beau, too." Maebry reluctantly let go of Gil's arm. It had been nice while it lasted. Shyly, she gazed up at him through her lashes, hoping to keep her feelings veiled. Her little crush on him wasn't as small as she tried to make herself believe.

"Oh, you two were *pretending?*" Gemma's voice sounded closer, maybe an aisle away. "I was about to say congratulations, but I get it now. That was a very clever way to foil Lawrence's advances."

"I had no choice. He came by the ranch yesterday evening to ask me out for a drive." Maebry rolled her eyes, trying to keep her tone light. She did feel sorry for Lawrence, but that wasn't the reason it felt as if the sunlight had gone out. "I had to say no to him in front of half the kitchen staff and the cowboys who'd wandered over to watch. It was awful. It was so terrible, wasn't it Gil?"

"No. You let him down as gently as you could. If I'd known you'd wanted a pretend beau, I could have stepped up and sent him on his way right there and then." Gil's baritone gentled. "It would have saved you from being uncomfortable."

"Thank you. I don't know why he's so persistent. He knows why I can't accept. *Not* that I would want to." She raised one shoulder up, then down, hoping the gesture would say what she could not. She felt Gil's gaze like a touch to her cheek, as if he were waiting for her to look up at him. For some reason she didn't want to, for that would make him suddenly too close, too intimate. She took a step away, fisted her hands, remembered the shopping list she was clutching. "You saved the day."

"I was only thinking of my stomach." A light quip, but the low dip of his tone said something more. Something that made her stomach clench up so tight it might never return to normal. "Not that you would have carried through with your threats."

"No, I really would have given you the burned pieces," she informed him, teasing. "I might have burned things on purpose just for you."

"Right, like I believe that." He winked at her, adjusted his hat, glanced out the window as if to make sure Lawrence had fled the scene for good. "You don't have a mean bone in your body, Maebry O'Riley. You were just bluffing."

"How do you know? Do I have to prove it to you?" She arched a brow at him. Sure, he was right, but a girl had to stand her ground, didn't she?

"We'll see come supper time." He gave a soft bark of laughter, his gaze finding hers. Warmth resonated in those dark blue depths and something mysterious, something she couldn't quite put her finger on. He dipped his chin, breaking eye contact and tipped his hat. "I'll be across the street if you lovely ladies need protecting."

"Lovely?" Maebry planted her hands on her hips. "Don't tell me that next you'll be turning into a Lawrence type."

"Well, it's a possibility." He winked, one big, capable hand curling around the door knob and engulfing it. "Maybe it could be the new me. I'd need a bowler hat, though."

"Take my advice. Do not trade in your Stetson."

"Okay, I'll keep that in mind." One corner of Gil's mouth tilted up into a half-grin, lopsided and dashing in a subtle, more masculine way that Lawrence on his best day could never hope to achieve. The bell above the door tinkled, announcing Gil's departure. He strode out the door, taking his very male presence with him.

"Whew, the store feels empty somehow when he leaves." Gemma swished into sight and held up the tin for inspection. "This is the tea you're after, right?"

"You know it. Maureen ran out again." Maebry grabbed a basket from the stack by the window and headed to inspect the packages of crackers. "She's having a rough time of it."

"I'm sorry to hear that." Gemma pushed a strand of black hair behind her ear and set the tea on the counter. "Rumor has it that she's having a hard time breathing."

"Yes, she's getting these weird episodes. Doc says she's near the end." Sad. Anyone's imminent passing was a sorrow, even Maureen's. Maebry's chest felt funny, tight with concern for the old lady even after all that had happened between them. She was family, after all, albeit distant. Very distant. "We're doing all we can to keep her comfortable."

"Hence the tea." Gemma's gait tapped lightly closer, her face genuinely concerned. "She's gone through the last tin so quickly. It must be one of the few comforts left to her."

"True." Maebry's gaze zipped across the store to the bank of front windows and the lone cowboy moseying across the dusty street. Back straight, long legs lean and strong, easy going stride. She didn't know why her throat closed up, making it hard to breathe. She could still feel the heat of his presence, the unyielding hardness of muscle and bone beneath her hand, the heat of his skin. Loneliness ached in her chest, which was foolish, really. She was twenty years old, she'd been on her own since she was fifteen, traveling from her home in Ireland by herself. She was alone and she accepted it. End of story.

But, still, her gaze lingered on the straight line of Gil's back. He was terribly fine. She couldn't help wishing, just a little, dreaming of him. Dreams couldn't hurt, right? She knew nothing could come of them, but the man just hooked her heart. There wasn't one thing she could do to stop it. But she had her duties and her obligations, and those came first.

And would for so many years, that it may as well be forever.

"He is a sight, isn't he?" Gemma plucked a tin of Maureen's favorite crackers from a nearby shelf, trying to hide a little sigh. "He's far too young for me, what is he, twenty-five, twenty-six? But still. My eyes can appreciate a fine man when he walks into my store."

"What, they weren't appreciating Lawrence?" Okay, perhaps it was wrong of her to tease. She chose a second tin of crackers from the shelf and plopped it into the wicker basket she'd hooked over her arm. "Sorry, I couldn't help it."

"We are sisters-in-arms, my dear." Gemma gave a helpless shrug and took the crackers out of Maebry's basket. "We have to stick together when it comes to that man. He is a trial."

"He's just lonely." The words seemed to scrape out of her throat, because she knew how that felt. She battled that feeling every single day when her work was done and she was alone in her little room off the kitchen, facing an endlessly lonely evening. "I feel bad for him."

"Not bad enough to let him beau you, I hope." Gemma set the crackers on the counter next to the tea. "Oh, he's harmless enough, but I don't think he'd make a good husband."

"Maybe none of them do," Maebry found herself saying, echoing the words her mother used, the same sentiment Maureen had expressed whenever she got the chance. Maebry winced, hoping that didn't mean she was on the verge of believing real love didn't exist, that true love was impossible. Or maybe it was a defense, instead of saying the truth. That she would likely never marry. Never have a husband to love, children to treasure.

Unwillingly, her eyes wandered toward the window again, catching the last glimpse of Gil as he yanked open the feed store's front door and ambled inside, out of sight. The sensation of the reassuring warmth of his arm pressed to hers lingered.

Maybe I'm just that hopeless, she thought with a head shake, consulted her crumpled list and marched down the nearest aisle.

* * *

Gil Blackburn ignored the drone of the chatter in the store as he hiked up to the front counter. He still felt a little dazed, but then Maebry O'Riley usually had that effect on him. Still, he thought, squaring his shoulders, it had felt good to help her, even if it had nearly broken his heart.

"Gil, good to see you." Carl Thomas, proprietor of this fine establishment, dusted hayseed off the scarred wooden counter. "What can I do you for?"

"We're running short on oats at the Rocking M." He splayed his hands on the edge of the counter, glancing over his shoulder at the mercantile across the street. The waning sun glinted too brightly on the windows to catch a glimpse of her. He cleared his throat. "Last year's twister wasn't good for our crops."

"Mine neither!" called Zeke Owens, cowboys sat in the far corner of the store, hunkered down on a feed barrel over a game of checkers.

"It stayed east of my place, I had a great harvest." Silas Meeks, his fellow player, jumped his red checker across the board, collecting black pieces. "Hey, Gil. Is it true? Are you courting Maebry?"

"What? How did you hear something like that?" He shook his head, guffawing, if only to cover the painful ache in his heart.

"Latimer came in to join our game," Zeke explained. "But we wouldn't let him."

Poor Lawrence. It wasn't his fault he was, well, the way he was. Gil felt sympathetic, since they were both clearly sweet on Maebry. The problem being that Lawrence was sweet on any female in town under forty.

"Yeah, what's the word, Gil?" Carl pulled out his accounts ledger and flipped through the pages. "Are you and Maebry serious?"

"What is with you all?" Gil glanced over his shoulder, straining to catch sight of her in the store. He simply needed to see her, but no luck. The sun dimmed, and all he could make out was the front window display showing off lady's shoes. "Do you really think a gal as pretty as Maebry O'Riley would settle for the likes of me?"

"Well, when you put it that way." Zeke winked, turned his attention to the game and pondered his next move. "Maebry would be foolish if she settled for you."

"Don't I know it?" Humor covered the painful truth. There was something wrong with him, letting his heart fix on a woman he couldn't have. Maebry had never shown a speck of interest in him, other than the friendliness she showed everyone. "We've worked together for a few months now. She knows me well enough to see faults and all. How can any lady get past that?"

"Exactly," Silas teased, wincing as he lost two checkers to Zeke. "Which is good for me. She doesn't know me yet. Think she'll have me?"

"Nah," Zeke added two checkers to his growing pile. "You're more faulty than Gil, and he doesn't stand a chance."

"Well, now, I disagree. Gil isn't so bad." Carl, a fatherly figure, reached for a pencil thoughtfully. "I'd reckon any number of ladies might think so too."

"Thanks, Carl." Gil took the pencil he offered, initialed the record of purchase and tipped his hat. "I appreciate it, but no woman has tied me down yet. Best to keep it that way."

"I understand, you like to roam free." Carl snapped the ledger closed, grinning easily. He was a kindly man, quiet, stocky but strong from years of lifting hundred and fifty pound sacks of grain in his store. Salt and pepper hair swirled around a thin spot on top where he was beginning to go bald, his angular face lined with laugh lines. Instead of making another friendly joke, his gaze turned serious, as if he somehow understood.

Revealed and not sure that he liked the storekeeper guessing his secret, Gil tipped his hat and headed for the stack of bagged oats. He hefted a bag over his shoulder, resisting the urge to turn around and check the mercantile windows one more time. It's impossible and you know that, he told himself as he headed out the door.

Something icy dove beneath his hat brim and brushed his cheek. He looked up. Snow. It hailed toward the ground in fat, thick flakes, *tap, tap, tapping* in every direction. The street turned white all around him.

"This is crazy!" A beautiful and familiar voice called from across the street. Maebry latched her wagon's tailgate and dusted the snow off her gloves. She peered at him from the depths of her hood, tattered and fraying in places, but her secondhand clothing could not dim her brightness. She shone like a beam of spring sunshine even in the darkening storm. "It's May!"

"It's Montana," he answered, somehow getting down the stairs without falling. Good thing his feet had found their way on his own, because all he really noticed was her. "You'd better head home before the roads get bad."

"Just what I was thinking." She spun on her heels, swishing away from him. Willowy and petite, she lifted her skirts, hopped up into the wagon and dusted off the snowy seat.

Nothing seemed to bother her. Not one thing. He absently bumped into something—the side of his own wagon—and dumped the bag of oats into the bed. The veil of snow threatened to cut off his view of her, but the wind gusted, allowing him one last look as she took the reins in her slender hands. Little wisps of sunshine blond hair tumbled down from her up knot to curl around her delicate, oval face. Emerald green eyes flashed as she laughed and raised one gloved hand to him in a graceful little wave.

"Thanks again for being my pretend beau," she called out as her wagon rattled by, drawn by one of the ranch's horses. "It may have been brief, but it was the best relationship I've ever had."

"Me, too." His heart took another wrench. Judging by her easygoing, friendly manner, she had no clue. Not a single one. He watched her roll away. "Get home safe!"

She was far enough away that he wasn't sure his words had reached her, but she fluttered her fingers in a little wave before the snow storm closed around her in a curtain of white, stealing her from his sight.

Something tugged on his sleeve. Casey, his bay gelding. Velvet lips clamped firmly on his coat cuff, dark eyes mildly reprimanding. Casey ran a tight ship, and he expected his master to do the same.

"All right, I'm done mooning." Gil scrubbed the horse's nose and jolted into action, pounding up the steps to the boardwalk, leaving a trail in the quickly accumulating white stuff. He couldn't help glancing over his shoulder one more time, wishing.

Wishing, when he had sacks of feed to bring home before this turned into a full-force blizzard. Tucking away his tender feelings for Maebry O'Riley, he buried them deep. Some things were simply not meant to be.

CHAPTER TWO

Stupid weather! Maebry swiped snow out of her face as she squinted at the disaster that had befallen the wagon. The ranch horse glanced over his shoulder at her, arched a horsy brow and sent her a worried look through the sideways falling snow.

"Phil, why are you looking at me like that?" She gave the wagon wheel a good hard kick. That was the old family rule. When frustrated, a good whack with your foot to whatever wasn't working never did any harm. Except to her toe, which protested painfully from smacking into the metal rim. "It's not my fault we're good and stuck."

Phil huffed, blowing air out of his nose.

"Okay, maybe it is a little," she admitted.

The horse stomped his foot, as if there was no *maybe* about it. Snow clung to his black mane giving him a frosty look. In fact, he was turning white all over, and so was she. Brrr. She wrapped her arms around herself, but nothing could stop the knife-sharp cut of the cruel northwestern wind as it sliced through her old coat.

"What I wouldn't give to be home right now in the toasty kitchen." Maebry took a step and felt the half-frozen mud clamp hold of her shoe. Ew. She tugged it free and frowned at the gooey mire of brown stuck to the sole. That would have to be washed off. "I can almost hear the tea kettle whistling on the stove. Wood crackling in the fire. Smell my beef stew simmering, my fresh bread baking."

As nice of an image as it was—and it did warm her up some—now her stomach decided to rumble. Great. She rolled her eyes, or she would have if snow wasn't driving into her face and she had to blink too hard to roll. Flakes clung to her eyelashes, smacked her cheeks, thudded on her nose. She squinted at the snowy wagon. No way was she getting the wheels free from the half-frozen mud, which had congealed to a nice sticky, paste-like mixture.

"Problem solved," she told Phil, taking a step toward him. "I'll just—"

She heard a pinging sound, her foot came free and icy air breezed between her toes. Oh, no! She glanced down, already knowing what she'd see. Her right shoe was sitting behind her all by its lonesome, stuck in the mud.

"Don't give me that look," she warned Phil. "This is my only pair of shoes."

Phil's brows arched higher, clearly doing his best not to utter a horsy laugh.

"Okay, so it is kind of funny." She stood there on one foot like a flamingo, wondering if she dared to try hopping back to her shoe. She tilted her head, considering. What if she hopped right out of her left shoe? Then where would she be?

A faint squeak of a wheel penetrated the chorus of wind and snow. She strained her ears, leaning into the gusts, hearing the jingling quality of harnessing. Yes! It was Gil on his way back to the ranch. She was saved. She bit her bottom lip, considering. Not that she would be saved from humiliation when he saw her standing on one foot like a lost bird, but maybe she could reward him with baked goods for fetching her shoe for her.

That put a grin on her face and a skip to her pulse. She twisted toward the road, searching the shadows for the first sight of him, for the hard, unyielding line of his shoulders, the no-nonsense silhouette of his hat and his hallmark, steely square jaw. Already looking forward to whatever amusing thing he might say with that butter-soft rumble to his smoky baritone, her pulse kicked up a crazy rhythm.

As she watched more eagerly than she cared to admit, a shadow did emerge from the white-gray curtain of the storm. Instead of a Stetson, she recognized the jolly shape of a bowler hat. Those slumped, almost straight shoulders and that handlebar mustache could only belong to one man. And it wasn't Gil. She tilted her head, desperate. Why wasn't it Gil? Her forehead scrunched up, her jaw tensed up, she let out a little gasp. Why did it have to be Lawrence Latimer?

"Miss Maebry." He pulled his donkey to a stop beside her. Sitting up straight in his cart, he tipped his hat, always a gentleman. His gaze went from her stockinged foot to the lone shoe in the road. "Allow me to come to your assistance, dear lady."

"Uh—" That was the only answer she had, the only word that tumbled off her tongue because her brain had entirely shut down in either shock or horror. She didn't know which. Maybe both, she considered, biting her lip harder.

"Let me fetch that for you." Lawrence wrapped his reins around the whip handle and hopped to the ground. "What are you doing out of your wagon in this weather? Oh, I see your wagon is stuck."

"Stuck," Maebry agreed helplessly. Just like she was. Stuck with him and not knowing how to begin to tell him no thank you, she'd rather stand like this until the rapture. "Perhaps you'd best get back in your cart. I wouldn't want you to get bogged down, too."

"Don't you worry, I kept high and center. I'm quite the experienced driver." He swaggered over to her shoe, bent to scoop it up most gallantly, only to be forced to tug a few times before it came free. "You popped off every single button. You'll need new shoes, I'm afraid."

"So I see." She reached out to snatch it from him, wishing more than anything it had been Gil who'd stopped, and feeling sorry for this man whose brown puppy-dog eyes shone with the hope to please. He gallantly knelt before her, and alarm shot through her. He was too close. Way too close. "What are you doing?"

"Putting on your shoe. A little like Cinderella, don't you think?" A question etched into his face as he stared up at her, ignoring the beat of snowflakes catching on his eyelashes. He bent his head to the task of upending the shoe and shaking any accumulated snow out of it. "You have two holes in your sock, Maebry. This shoe has been patched so often, the patches have patches. If anyone is in need of a prince charming, it's you."

And she suspected what Lawrence was really saying is that he was the one in need of a Cinderella, of someone to fill the loneliness and emptiness in his life. Her heart twisted in sympathy, because she knew how that felt.

"Really, that's kind of you, Lawrence." She hiked up her chin, taking care to keep her voice gentle. "But I don't need a prince charming. I'm the kind of girl who puts her own shoe on, thank you, so please hand it over."

"Oh, if you're sure." His face fell. Disappointment etched onto his long, narrow face for one moment, as he thought it all over, then shrugged sheepishly. "Guess I already knew that, especially now that you're with Gil and all. That must be why I like you so much. You're independent, and that's a strength in a woman as beautiful as you are."

Stop already, she thought, biting her lip to keep from laughing. Really, what did it take? He'd already gotten the hint, in fact he understood her quite well, but did that stop him? No. She rolled her eyes heavenward, batting her eyelashes against the constant barrage of snowflakes, remembering to count to ten.

"I should help you with your wagon." Lawrence straightened his narrow shoulders, handing over her shoe. A thin note of hope rang in his words and hitched both eyebrows up in big, hairy arches. "Or perhaps I could offer you a ride?"

"No, thank you." Maebry clenched her back teeth, a bit frustrated. He had persistence, she had to give him that. "It was really nice of you to stop and offer assistance. Very gentlemanly."

"Well, I try." He knocked snow off the narrow brim of his bowler, looking her straight in the eye, for he was barely an inch taller than she was. "Guess I'll see you at the Montgomery's party, but keep me in mind. You know, if things don't work out with you and Gil. I mean, I have enough money to buy out your contract with Maureen, just something you might want to know."

"Oh. Well, Maureen won't cash me out, she's made that terribly clear." Her throat closed, cutting off her words. No one but Maureen—and she suspected Maureen's daughter Aumaleigh—knew the reason she was in such insurmountable debt. It wasn't enough that she was an indentured servant to Maureen, but she'd borrowed money too. Money that would take almost a decade of daily work to pay off.

Thinking of her little sister, her chin hiked up. It was worth it. "You are truly kind to stop, Lawrence. We'd both better get home before we freeze into icicles."

"Right." Lawrence planted his feet. "At least lean on me while you put on that shoe. No lady falls on my watch."

THEN CAME YOU

"Well, I—" She hesitated, not knowing what to say, when a dark looming shadow broke free from the veil. He dominated the storm, emerging from it as if the fury of wind and snow dared not touch him. Her pulse skipped a beat or two—likely from surprise, she thought, and not anything else like, say, complete and total happiness at seeing him.

"I'll take it from here, Latimer." Gil's deep tone held friendliness, but the low notes rang with an unspoken warning. "Thanks for stopping to help."

"S-sure. My pleasure." Lawrence paled again, terribly small when compared to the hulking cowboy. The little man tipped his bowler cordially and backed away toward his cart. "Couldn't drive by and leave a lady in distress."

"Right." Gil tipped his hat cordial but remote-looking, as expressionless as a rock. Hard to figure out what he was thinking.

Probably wondering why I'm standing here like a heron, she thought as Lawrence disappeared into the storm. Embarrassed, she lifted her stockinged foot to try and stick it into the shoe she held.

"Here, let me." Suddenly Gil was there, his big body blocking her from the wind. His gloved hand ripped the shoe from her grip and he knelt before her. "I can't have you falling over."

"I was never in danger of falling over."

"Still, it's my cowboy's duty to help those in need."

"I think that means the hungry or the downtrodden." Her face flamed, because he'd hit a sore spot. Aware of the worn state of her clothes, she slipped her foot into her shoe, held so steady in his hands. It felt terribly intimate somehow, personal and close. Perhaps because she could feel the warmth radiating from him. Not that she wanted to acknowledge any feelings she might have—say, feelings that went beyond a mere passing crush on the man. Her chin hiked up. "I'm hardly either."

"Well, you *do* have two holes in that stocking." Gentle that tone, caring. His hat hid his face as he lowered her foot to the ground.

Her cheeks flamed, but his gentleness helped ease her humiliation. He'd worked at the ranch since February. He knew about her situation, that she was Maureen's indentured servant and earned no wages. Everything she earned went straight to paying off her debt. She'd prepared and served his meals every day, along with the rest of the ranch hands, so her life was no secret to him. Perhaps it was the understanding—and the embarrassment of being so destitute—that made her eyes sting.

"I know, I've been feeling those holes in my sock all morning long." Humor, she thought. That's what she needed. Gil felt extraordinarily close, even as he stood up, rising to his impressive, towering height. She could not afford to let down her guard. "Guess I have some darning to do tonight."

"Seems like that stocking has been patched up one too many times." The caring in his voice reached out to her, made her look up when she wanted to look away, made her lean in just a fraction of an inch when she'd be smart to leap away.

"Yes, and exactly what were you doing looking that closely at my stocking?" She hiked up an eyebrow, trying to go back to the usual, casual banter that had always naturally existed between them. Feared that she couldn't. "Perhaps you could answer that?"

"Hey, I couldn't help myself." The hint of his smile returned. "You have a pretty foot."

"Seriously? You're going to try and charm me? You're no better than Lawrence."

"Maybe, maybe not." The faint smile vanished from his rugged face, the corners of his mouth tipped downward. He was serious, there was no more light-heartedness between them as he stepped back into the snow, disappearing into it. When he spoke, his voice came muffled by the storm, drifting to her on a wintry wind. "I know it doesn't look like it now, but I've been really poor too."

"When?" Her forehead crinkled, her chest tugged with surprise and concern. Gil had hired on after George Klemp was fired. Gil was second in command at the Rocking M, so capable and obviously successful at what he did. He had one of the nicest horses of all the hired men. "It had to be long ago."

"After my folks died when I was ten, I lived in an orphanage for a couple of years." Matter of fact, those words, holding no emotion.

She wished the storm wasn't between them, that she could see his face, read what he wasn't saying in his eyes. She hadn't known this about Gil. In fact, she knew very little about him. She'd rarely been alone with him before this. There was always someone else around in the Rocking M kitchen or on the ranch, or even in town.

THEN CAME YOU

"I'm sorry, Gil. That had to have been devastating." She shivered as the wind buffeted her, penetrating the layers of her clothing, chilling her to the skin. "My da died when I was thirteen. Still had my mother, but she remarried soon after."

"Let me guess. He was no decent man." Gil reappeared, swathed in snow, iron strong. "That's why you left Ireland so young, to escape."

"Yes." She had memories of those dark times she kept under lock and key. They were behind her, why bring them out in the light now? Her stepfather could no longer harm her or her sister. What was years of servitude and debt when compared with that? "But we were talking about you. Were you adopted?"

"In a way, I guess. My uncle finally came to claim me." He might have been talking about anything—the weather, gossip, the new building under construction in town—instead of the pain in his life. He pulled a length of twine from his pocket. "He was a brute of a man. Something we have in common."

She felt sucker punched. She never would have guessed it, that Gil had known the sting of a brutal man's violence. As Gil knelt down before her, a big, powerful man on the ground at her feet, a lump lodged in her throat. Swallowing hard didn't remove it completely. She let the silence settle between them. His confession felt too intimate, as if they were both without defenses and shields, revealed to each other. It wasn't a feeling she liked or was used to.

"When I was doing time in that orphanage, that's when I was poor. Not enough food, clothes handed down until they were rags. Oh, the place did their best. It wasn't intentional." Gil's gloved hands quickly banded the twine around her ankle, wrapping it snugly. "It was worse with my uncle. I ran off when I was fourteen. Lived on my own for weeks. Slept in fields, ate roots and berries when I could find them. I'd go to bed so hungry I couldn't sleep while my stomach gnawed on itself."

"Gil." Sympathy swamped her. It burned in her eyes, filled her to overflowing. It was hard to imagine him as a boy, not yet a man, alone and suffering. "I've been that hungry back in Ireland."

"It takes one to know one." His words reached out to her like a touch, bridging the distance between them. Still kneeling down, the crown and brim of his Stetson hid his face. Her eyes traced the rigid set of his shoulders and back, the muscled length of his arms. He was invincible. Always in a good mood, easy going, he seemed as if his life had always been that way.

You just never knew what someone else's path has been, she reminded herself, unable to stop her hand from reaching out, somehow needing to touch him, and landing on the outer curve of his upper arm. He felt like a mountain come to life, so solid, so real.

"I wish things had been easier for you," she said lightly, but she didn't remove her hand from his arm. There were things she couldn't say, things she shouldn't even be feeling, and she somehow wanted him to know that. As if she hoped he could sense it in her touch or read it in her eyes. And even if he couldn't, her fingers wanted to stay on his arm.

Not that she had the right to hold on.

"Hey, things are good for me." He tied the ends of the twine into a bow, neatly binding her shoe to her. "I found a good job as a stable boy, I worked hard, saved my money and worked my way up. Even earned enough to buy Casey."

From somewhere in the storm, a horse blew out his breath in a horsy comment.

"Best money I ever spent," Gil said, pitching his voice as if to make sure his gelding heard it. With a grin, Gil stood, rising up to block the wind and snow. "It turned out all right. But what about you?"

"I'm grateful to Maureen. It's turned out all right for me too." So much better than her life had been in Ireland, that was for sure. The only regret she had was that she was not free, her life was not her own. Maureen owned a contract on her and it had to be paid. "I'm thankful every day."

"For being an indentured servant?" His sculpted mouth hooked up in one corner, an almost smile the rest of his mouth didn't complete. Something serious flickered in his vivid gaze, but it was hard to tell because of the snow hurling down between them. When she looked again, that seriousness was gone, but the air felt changed.

She felt changed. As if they were closer somehow than before.

"It's not so bad." She took a step to test the integrity of the twine-and-shoe combination. It seemed to work. "I have job security, for one thing. No matter what, I'll always be employed."

"True. Unlike me, you don't have to worry about being fired." Gil's humor returned as he moved to her side.

"Exactly!" How nice it felt when he ushered her through the snow, protecting her from the brunt of the wind with his big body, making sure she didn't fall. "I have room and board provided for years to come. No worries there."

"That sounds like a bonus."

"Oh, it is. I work with great people."

"Yep, great. That's me."

"Not you," she corrected, mischievously. "But some great people."

"Good to know where I stand." His wagon rose out of the storm, hulking and shadowed. He gripped her arm, helped her up. "At least I'm not in the Lawrence category."

"Don't be too sure about that." The wind gusted ever harder, drowning out his chuckle, driving the straight-line snow with the wind speed of a twister. She clearly struggled to stay upright as she swiped snow from the wagon seat. "All you'd need is a handlebar mustache and you'd be twins."

"Now that's where you'd be wrong." Light, humorous, he helped with the snow swiping. A few brushes and the wagon seat was as clear as it was going to get. "I'll go fetch your groceries and the horse. Can you stay out of trouble while I'm gone?"

"I can try." She plopped down onto the wagon seat, covered with snow, her face scoured pink from the cold. She'd let her muffler slip down.

He reached over to tug it up, tenderness kicking in his chest. The curve of her face was so dear, so delicate and sweet. Her big emerald green eyes shone brightly as if with their own light, hinting at her inner beauty. It would be nice if she was his to care for, he thought, arranging the worn muffler higher on her shoulders, around her throat, to better shield her face. He'd cherish her. He'd make sure she was happy, or die trying.

Not that she realized he felt that way. The caring he felt was not reflected in her stunning green eyes, was not returned to him, so he backed away.

"Don't garner any more suitors while my back is turned, okay?" he joked, if only to hide the ache of gentleness that surged through his chest.

"I'll try," she teased back. "But no promises."

When he walked away from her amused smile, the warmth of it

stayed with him even in the worsening storm. Well, his affections for her kept deepening, even though this was a one-sided thing. He plowed through the accumulating snow, sloshed through the sticky mud and spotted the shadow of a horse through the tumbling downfall.

"Hey there, Phil." He greeted the horse he knew well, for all of the cowboys lately took turns tending the ranch horses and cleaning stalls. Times were lean at the Rocking M, and several hired hands had already walked off the job for lack of pay. He patted the gelding's nose. "Bet you thought we'd forgotten about you, huh?"

Phil nickered, pressing gratefully against the palm of Gil's hand. The poor animal was coated with snow, looking a little forlorn, hitched to the mired-down wagon.

"No way would I forget about you." He assured the animal, gave him a final nose stroke and got down to the business of unbuckling and leading Phil out of his traces. The storm didn't make it easy.

His thoughts turned back to Maebry, and the protective fury—okay, call it jealousy—he'd felt when he'd found her alone with Latimer. Lawrence had no call trying to court her. Lawrence was new to town, he'd bought a patch of land next to the Rocking M, not even four months ago. Anger roared through him as Gil slogged down the road.

Two months and seven days. That's how long he'd been in love with Maebry. His jaw clenched tight, his molars grinding together as he stopped beside Casey. When he squinted up into the storm, she was nothing but a silhouette—a curve of her hood, the bow of her head against the storm, the elegant line of her sleeve as she braced herself on the seat.

As he bent to buckle Phil in next to Casey, he remembered the first day he saw her. It had been a dreary March day, a mantle of thick, charcoal clouds shrouded the sky, the rolling hills and fields of the ranch were frozen but snowless. He'd dismounted outside a two-story log house, teeth chattering from the ride, frozen to the marrow of his bones. He'd been gathering Casey's reins when movement caught his eye. There, in the window, stood the most beautiful woman he'd ever seen. Golden hair like liquid sunshine, porcelain skin, angelic beauty that made his heart skip to a stop. Transfixed, his soul sighed as if in wonder, and when she laughed, he could feel it lilting inside him.

Determination filled him now. He patted the horses, straightened up, resisting the tug of longing within. He'd been waiting all this time for her to notice him. For her to realize that the little things he did for her—bringing in wood, fetching water, making sure she had the most reliable horse on the ranch for her trips into town—had nothing to do with his job. But because he loved her.

And that's why he would see her safely home. He would do everything he could for her, hoping one day she would take a good long look and see him differently, see a man she could love.

CHAPTER THREE

"Too bad the storm didn't hold off until sundown, the way you cowboys predicted." Maebry's teeth chattered behind her woolen muffler, trying to ignore the affect of Gil's presence as she swept snow off the wagon seat for him. "I'd have worn my winter long johns."

"Me, too." He dropped down beside her, taking command of the reins. An abominable snowman would have been less snowy. White clung to him everywhere—the brim of his hat, his eyebrows, his muffler wrapped loosely around his throat. He gave the reins a snap. "I don't even have a horse blanket to offer you. Are you doing okay? You're not too cold, are you?"

"I'm tougher than I look." Her spine straightened. She had to be. "Besides, we're almost home."

"True, but that might be easier said than done." He pulled up his muffler one handed, as the wagon rocked forward cautiously in the heavy accumulation. The snow pounded down so thick and furious that you couldn't see the horses at all. "This is going to get interesting."

"Keep high and center." She smiled against the scratchy wool of her muffler. "At least that's what Lawrence told me."

"Funny." He leaned into the storm, as if to will them through. "Any more driving advice you want to give? It takes a certain skill to get a wagon stuck that badly."

"It was the snow." Why did she always want to laugh when she was in this man's presence? It was a total mystery. She should be too frozen to talk, she should be upset about the wagon—she knew Maureen was going to have a fit if she heard about it—plus the fact that her attempts to thwart Lawrence's interest in her had backfired, making the whole situation worse. He'd offered to try to pay off Maureen! Craziness.

"Sure, it was the snow. That was the reason," Gil teased gently. "It wasn't your driving."

"Glad you understand." She smiled against her muffler, feeling her breath begin to freeze to the coarse wool. "The road was all white, so I couldn't see the mud."

"A likely story." Humor rumbled through him, his chuckle warm as stove-top molasses. Caring resonated in his eyes.

Caring.

Honest and unguarded. Something she'd never noticed before.

"You look cold," he observed.

"Yes, as it's well below freezing." She tried to smile, but she wasn't sure her mouth was working properly. Probably because she was mesmerized by him. Surprised at the unexpected realization of how Gil felt.

How he really shouldn't be feeling. Her chest ached with a strange sorrow. Because it was one thing to have a crush on a man when you knew your heart was safe. It was another to see that caring reflected back at you. She stared straight ahead into the storm, seeing only whiteness. It would have been better if she'd never seen caring in his eyes. Much easier.

Somehow the fact that nothing could ever come of his feelings was worse. Gil knew that her life was not her own. It wouldn't be until she was almost thirty, too many years for a man to wait, even if he was interested.

Best to pretend she'd never noticed the caring in his gaze. She bowed her head, stared down at her gloved hands. "I'm not cold at all."

"Your teeth are chattering."

"No, they are just bumping together because the road is bumpy."

"A likely story." He inched over, closing the distance between them on the bench seat, driving out all awareness of the storm, until there was only his hulking manliness, just his closeness, his tantalizing warmth. "Maureen knew about the bad weather coming, I know Beckett told her about it. She shouldn't have sent you out in this. It's too cold for a lady."

"I'm not a lady. I'm an indentured servant." Her chin went up. She had her dignity, if not her freedom. She'd traded seven years of her life for passage here to escape the misery of poverty, for a new hope for her life. A better beginning. She'd traded another seven so her sister could have the same. "I'm tougher than I look."

"Sure you are. That's why you needed my help chasing off Lawrence today."

"And I thanked you, right? By the way, you are a wonderful pretend beau and you make a really good wind block."

"Glad I'm good for something." His voice dipped low, as if there was something more there than simple humor. "Don't forget you promised baked goods."

"Did I? I can't remember." There, that made him laugh, and she laughed too, resisting the sweet tug on her heart that made her want to turn her gaze to him, to drink in every detail of this man and his kindness. Good thing she kept her eyes focused squarely on her gloves and the fraying strand of yarn that needed mending.

"Hey, don't pretend to forget. We made a deal. If you don't deliver a plate of cookies, maybe I'll haul you over to Lawrence myself." Humor, rumbling in his voice, gentle in his tone, tugged her toward him, so that her body was leaning against her will, her gaze tracked over the granite planes of his handsome face and she couldn't stop. It felt as if her heart had come open like a long locked window. How was she going to convince herself she didn't feel a thing for Gil now?

"Come here." His arm came around her shoulders, strong and comforting, and he drew her protectively against him. It felt as if he wanted to protect her from more than the storm.

Was it wrong to lean in, to snuggle into his solid heat? She couldn't seem to stop herself. He felt so good. As she cuddled against his side, his arm came around her like an iron band. Squished comfortably against him with her cheek resting against his chest, she listened to the reliable *thump-thump* of his heart. As if that wasn't intimate enough, as if they were not close enough, he tipped his hat low and bowed in, so his Stetson protected her eyes and the uncovered part of her face from flying snow. Wow. Never had anything felt as nice as being held by him.

Emotion pricked behind her eyes. She'd never, well, *felt* so much. It didn't help that she'd figured out the truth about Gil, how he felt about her. And she couldn't let that knowledge change a thing. Maureen would never allow her to be courted, she'd never give her enough time off to date. With a wistful sigh, she thought of the debt she still owed Maureen, not yet half-way paid off. It was a contract that would not end with Maureen's death, which according to the doctor would be sooner rather than later. No, this was a debt Maureen could always sell to the highest bidder or could leave to her heir. Even more likely, the contract would be sold by the attorney to help pay for Maureen's debts and funeral costs, and who knew where she would be forced to go then or who she'd be legally obligated to work for.

So no, it was better not to let her feelings get carried away. Best to be sensible about this. Gently, reluctantly, she pulled away from Gil's side, from his shelter and comfort. It was the sensible thing to do. Best to keep things friendly. That's the way it had to be.

But it wasn't what she wanted. Nothing was harder than shimmying out of Gil's arms and scooting several inches away from him. She let the winds batter her, felt the relentless snow slap and strike her. On the seat beside her, Gil said nothing. He simply switched the reins into both hands and didn't look her way.

Maybe he'd come to the same conclusion, too.

* * *

"Here we are." Gil's voice reached out to her. He gestured toward a faint shadow passing overhead. The entrance sign to the ranch. "Almost home. How are you doing?"

"Good." Well, not great, but she didn't want him to know that. Feeling very lonesome on her end of the wagon seat, she wrapped her arms around herself, trying to keep her body heat in. Wasn't working well, since her teeth kept chattering harder. The warmth and comfort she'd felt by his side taunted her.

If she crept over to him, it would be a mistake. The door to her heart stood open, and she had to find a way to close it. Her chest smarted with a deep, unrelenting ache. He fell silent again as they jostled along blindly in the storm. She listened to the sounds of the horses struggling—their heavy breathing, their uneven gait, the protesting squeal of the wagon wheels on the snowy slope. She couldn't help worrying. What if Gil didn't understand why she'd pulled away? What if he thought she didn't like him and hadn't wanted his comfort?

She choked at the thought, hiding the cough in the icy-crust of her muffler. When she cut her gaze sideways, he sat stoic at his end of the board seat like the tough cowboy he was, head bowed to the storm, determined to get them through. A man anyone could count on. She gave a little wistful sigh.

Why wasn't she stronger than this? Unhappy with herself for wishing for what she could not have, she tried to close that open place in her heart. The place that felt so sore, wished for so much. Gil pulled back on the reins.

"Whoa." The wagon rocked to a stop and the faint, tantalizing glint of lamplight flickered through the pelting snow. "We're home, safe and sound."

"So we are." She recognized the distant tone to his voice, hated that she had put it there. She had to, what choice did she have? Even if Gil *did* like her, if he was a little sweet on her, then she could not encourage him. It wouldn't be right. As much as it hurt, she planted her feet on the floorboards and hauled her partly-frozen, very stiff body upward until she was standing. "Thanks for the ride and the rescue. You make a pretty good pretend beau."

"I'll be happy to step in anytime you need it." He rose up to full height, his hand cupping both her elbows, drawing her forward with him. Closer to him. "Say, at the Montgomery's May Day party. Lawrence is determined when it comes to you."

"I have no idea why he would be. Honestly." She gasped when his hands trailed down her arms like a caress. Even through the layers of wool and cloth, her skin tingled. "There are other single ladies around."

"Not many," Gil corrected, backing to the edge of the wagon and stepping down with a powerful, masculine grace. "If women around here are single, they tend to get snatched up pretty quick."

"Still, a man wouldn't have to pay out a small fortune for them." There, she hoped her message would get across. He stood unblinking with his hat brim back, his bright blue eyes searching hers. As if he understood her meaning, he nodded once, winced as if in acknowledgement.

There. At least he understood what she could not say. She was glad for that. No man, no one, was going to go to such extremes for her.

And she wouldn't want them to. She bobbed her head, sure of it. Even if the open place in her heart squeezed with feeling, sore with both sadness and gratitude. For a moment back there on the ride home, she'd felt free, unfettered by the contract that dictated her life. Spending time with a man she liked, being held by him. It was a moment to cherish.

But it was over. She placed her hands in his larger ones and stepped down from the wagon. Weightless, she hung suspended in air for one brief moment, aware of his muscled strength as he lowered her toward the ground. Her shoes hit the snowy earth, but her heart felt airborne.

"You need to know something, Maebry O'Riley." Gil tugged at her hood, straightening it to better protect her eyes from the snow. "You would be worth a small fortune. Wait, even a large one."

"No." She blushed at the sincere dip of his words, of how they rumbled with truth and caring. "That's not true, I—"

He leaned in, pulled down an edge of her muffler and pressed a kiss to her cheek. She drew in air, surprised, dazed, confused. Unexpected sweetness, that kiss. The exposed place in her heart she could not close eked open a little more. She'd never dared to let herself dream of this moment, when the crush she had on him turned to something more.

"Just practicing." He re-adjusted her muffler, brushing off snow, tugging it back up. "I mean, we have to make this convincing if we're going to be a pretend couple."

"Isn't that taking it a little far?" Her hands lifted upward without thought, as if aching to land on the impressive span of his chest. She caught herself in time, pulling back. A little wistful, wishing she'd touched him. Instead, she steeled her spine and took a step back. "We don't have to convince everyone."

"Oh, I don't mind." Tender. The timbre of his voice, the curve of his mouth, the glint in his eyes that studied her intently, as if trying to look inside her. "I keep my promises. When I agree to do something, it's one hundred and ten percent."

"That is the problem with you, Gil." Her fingers moved of their own accord, she could not stop them as they landed on his forearm, touching him, connecting with him. "You're a good guy."

"Well, fair to middling." He reached for something behind her. The grocery crate. He tucked it into the crook of his arm, as if it weighed nothing. "We'd better get you in. Can't leave the horses standing in this wind."

"You go on and take care of them." Knowing it was the right thing to do, she wrestled the crate from him. Putting distance between them was the smartest thing to do. "You're right, they've worked up a sweat getting us safely here. They come first. I can see myself to the door."

"What did I just tell you? Remember the one hundred and ten percent thing?" Something mysterious shadowed his eyes, when the rest of him was smiling.

She soaked in the sight of his smile. Crinkles and manly lines, the craggy cut of his cheekbones, the good-guy look of him. *Thud*, went her heart, falling just a little bit more. If she wasn't careful, this crush she felt was going to balloon into doom. So she took a step back, giving him no choice. "Save it for the May Day party, cowboy. I'm an independent lady."

"Except for the indentured thing." His grin dimmed a notch, because he had to know she was rejecting him again. His shoulders went back, as if determined. "You can't be independent and indentured at the same time."

"I was talking about my personality." She rolled her eyes. Was he feeling this way too, as if he didn't want this to end, as if he didn't want to let go?

"You should work on your personality then." Twinkles returned to his eyes. "Might want to rethink that independent thing."

"No, what I'm wanting is more of it." Her shoe found the first porch step and she stumbled up onto it. Drawn to him, wishing she wasn't, she glanced over her shoulder. Big man, bigger personality. She steeled her heart, trying to resist him. "It keeps me safe from men like you."

"Like me?" All innocence, hands on his hips, feet braced, his grin widening. "Well, that's all the proof I need. You're sweet on me, Maebry O'Riley. I knew it."

"You know nothing." She edged up onto the next step, wishing he didn't know the truth. Best to deny it. "I'm not interested in you, Gilbert Blackburn."

"I know what I saw." Teasing her now, but he really wasn't teasing.

"Sorry, but you need glasses, Mister. You saw incorrectly."

"There's nothing wrong with my eyesight. And don't think I'm going to forget about your promises."

"What promises?" Best to feign ignorance than to turn around right now, she thought, slogging across the snowy porch.

"Baked goods," he called out, nothing but a shadow in the white downpour now. "No cold or burned things on my supper plate."

"Hmm, I don't seem to recall making that deal." With a laugh, she shifted the crate to her left arm, balancing it against her side, and turned the door knob. It was simply too easy to joke with him. "You should pay better attention when we talk, Gil. Men simply do not listen."

"Right." The whiskey-smooth cadence of his laughter carried on the wind, as personal as a touch, as soul-melting as his kiss. The wind gusted, stealing him from her sight. But a ribbon of connection remained, something so sweet and bright not even the storm could break it.

You are in big trouble, Maebry. She bowed her head, gave the knob a twist and stepped into the light and warmth of the Rocking M's kitchen house. Once the original homestead, it was now headquarters for all the ranch's cooking. Three meals a day were prepared for the three dozen cowboys that lived and worked on the Rocking M.

The minute she closed the door behind her, she felt the laughter within her dim. For a moment, she'd forgotten herself again, laughing with a guy she liked, feeling cozy because he seemed to like her back. But she could not be that girl. She set the crate on the nearby counter, unwrapped her muffler and smiled at the other women in the room.

"Goodness, look at you." Aumaleigh rushed across the ranch's warm kitchen, her lovely, heart-shaped face crinkled with concern. In middle-age, Aumaleigh managed to hold onto her beauty, although these days she did look worn from the struggle to take care of her mother. Her blue eyes gentled with concern. "You must be frozen clean through. Come right over here and warm up by the stove. Josslyn, draw up a chair."

"No, I'm fine," Maebry argued, dreading the uproar to come if she wasn't doing her duty by serving Maureen. "Don't bother with me. Not when there's tea to serve."

"Right." Josslyn set a steaming tea kettle on a trivet on the big work table in the center of the large kitchen. Middle age looked good on her too, her red hair was only lightly touched with gray. "You got here just in time. I was just about to brew a pot of her second favorite tea, since it's four o'clock on the dot."

"Whew. Just in the nick of time." Maebry hung up her muffler and unbuttoned her coat. "Oh, I brought her favorite crackers, too."

"Excellent." Josslyn dove into the crate, finding the new tin of tea just as a hand bell rang from an upstairs room. Josslyn frowned. "That would be her."

"I'll get the crackers." Strain paled Aumaleigh's face as she spoke over the bell. "Hurry, Josslyn. Are you sure you want to serve her, Maebry?"

"It's my job, right?" She whipped off her coat, forcing her mind to cut off all thoughts of Gil. To resist searching for him through the whitely hazed window. Whatever she felt for Gil, it was not real life. More like a daydream.

"Aumaleigh, use that plate." Josslyn scrambled to spoon tea leaves into the steeping ball. "Hurry."

"Thanks." Aumaleigh pried open the cracker tin and set several out on the plate, arranging the tray, fetching a sugar bowl and a spoon while Josslyn dropped the ball into the pot and poured the water.

"Sorry about the snow tracks." Maebry rushed across the room a little squishily and grabbed the tray Josslyn shoved at her. The bell jangled again, sharp and insistent. Angry this time.

"Maebry!" An elderly woman scolded from upstairs, her tone irritated and sharp enough to pierce wood. "I hear you down there, you lazy girl. Get up here. Bring my tea."

"Coming!" Maebry dove toward the stairs in the hallway, the teacup rattling in its saucer with every step. She charged upstairs, her pulse *rat-tat-tatting* partly panic because she really didn't want to endure Maureen's wrath, but that wasn't the only reason. In truth her heart hadn't beat normally since Gil had kissed her cheek.

He'd kissed her! It felt as if she'd left her heart behind, out there in the storm with him.

"Hurry up, you!" Maureen reprimanded. "I've had just about enough of waiting for you. Much more of this, and I'll sell your contract to the highest bidder, hire me a maid who can do her duty. I swear I will."

"Sorry, ma'am." Maebry tripped down the hall and into the room, where Maureen lay in bed, propped up by pillows. Her limbs gnarled and wasted, she was a skeleton in fine clothes. A scowling skull.

Sympathy for the dying woman filled her. She set the tray on the bedside table.

"Don't sorry me," Maureen snapped, struggling to lift her one good arm to point a gnarled finger. "You jump when I say jump, and you bring my tea on time. I own you, girl, you do what I say. Do you understand me?"

"Yes." She nodded, dutifully. Maureen wasn't wrong and she had the signed contract to prove it.

Maebry's hand shook as she poured the tea, the steaming, fragrance scenting the room. The fire snapping in the nearby hearth chased away the storm's chill as she stirred in a lump of sugar and held up the cup to Maureen.

"It's too hot," Maureen barked, screwing up her wrinkled face like a prune. Hard eyes silently rebuked, silently judged.

"Sorry." Maebry blew on the tea gently, grabbed the spoon and stirred a few times. "There, that looks better."

"Too cool." Maureen didn't look at the cup. "Heat it up."

Biting back her frustration, Maebry poured a few inches of tea into the nearby empty wash basin and topped the cup, added a fraction of a sugar cube, stirred and blew. "This feels right."

"It had better be." Maureen sneered as she held up her weak, gnarled hand for her tea.

Biting her lip, enduring the threat, Maebry made sure the old lady had a good hold on the cup before she let go. Maureen struggled to lift the cup to her lips. Her hand shook, while the other lay motionless at her side. It was a sad sight, to see her fight so hard, leaning forward toward the cup unsteadily, while tea threatened to slosh over the side and scald her.

Full of pity, Maebry gently steadied the bottom of the cup, supporting it so Maureen could feel as if she was doing it all herself, when she wasn't. She took a tentative sip, a little swallow and tea drooled down from one corner of her mouth. Maebry wordlessly grabbed a napkin from the tray and dabbed Maureen's lips.

"Don't you look at me like that." The old lady drew up her lips, sneering. "I don't need your pity, you worthless girl, but believe you me. You're going to need mine. I want the entire upstairs scrubbed clean. Floors, ceilings, walls. Everything. Before you go to bed tonight."

"Yes, ma'am." She sighed, resigned. She'd given up the right to be upset at the injustice of it long ago. All it took was one thought of Nia happy in Dakota Territory, working as a governess to three little girls. That was worth anything.

Real love was sacrifice, as she'd learned from her mother, as she was learning from her life. She was glad of her decisions, although they limited her future. As she steadied Maureen's cup while the old woman struggled with another sip, Maebry closed the door to her heart, the one Gil had opened.

From now on, it had to stay shut.

CHAPTER FOUR

Felt like the blizzard was blowing itself out. Gil set down his book, hopped off the straw bale he used for a chair and let himself out of Casey's stall. The gelding snoozed, breathing softly, lost in dreams. Latching the gate quietly so as not to wake his best buddy, Gil's thoughts turned back to Maebry. She hadn't served supper tonight. He'd even checked out the kitchen, but she hadn't been there either.

Maybe that's a sign. He sighed, fetched his book and turned down the lantern hanging on a center post, until only darkness remained. On second thought, maybe he shouldn't have kissed her cheek. That had to be the reason why she was avoiding him.

Why had he done such a rash thing? He blew out a sigh, frowning, ambling down the dark main aisle. She'd pulled away from him. Wasn't that another glaring, unmistakable clue? But no, he'd had to move in when anyone else would have gotten the hint. His chest cinched, full of longing for her, proof of how powerfully he felt.

The barn's silence surrounded him. Horses in their stalls, fast asleep, even the barn cats were dozing. This was his favorite time of night, when the ranch hands were up at the bunkhouse, the animals safe and fed and cared for. The barn was far cozier than hanging out in the bunkhouse with a bunch of jaded cowboys. And it was a far sight closer to the kitchen house where Maebry worked and lived.

Maebry. He winced, tucked his book on his shelf in the tackroom and reached for his muffler and gloves. This time of night, she'd be reading in her little room off the kitchen. He knew because she'd always smile and wave to him when he came in with an armload of firewood. Sometimes she'd even come out and exchange a few polite words with him.

Polite. That was the key word, the important one he had to pay attention to. He bowed his head, looping the muffler around his neck, unable to ignore the foolish feeling rising up. The last thing he wanted was to look like Lawrence Latimer, not knowing when to back off. A little sheepish, he rubbed a hand over his face, tired, a little heartsick. That kiss to her cheek had been a mistake, especially if she was avoiding him.

Well, he owed her an apology at the least. His pride stung, but he'd do right by her. She shouldn't have to go around tomorrow worrying about avoiding him, too, right? Right. His chest felt hollow as he buttoned up his coat all the way and reached for his gloves. Looked like he didn't have a chance with her. That hurt.

Disappointed, his foot stumbled on his way to the door, but he kept going. Headed out into the storm, head bowed, full of determination. Icy pellets walloped him, a mean wind tried to blow him off course, but he kept going until he found the snow-covered woodpile against the kitchen house. He filled his arms full and hiked to the back door. The weather was brutal, but he kept going. Even if she would never be his, he wouldn't stop doing things for her.

He just couldn't.

Gritting his teeth, trying to keep his feelings as frozen as the outside world, he wrestled open the back door and tumbled into the dark kitchen. The faint scents of the day's cooking lingered in the air, buttermilk bread, peppery beef stew, molasses baked beans. A lamp in the hallway tossed enough light into the room for him to see by. As he moseyed toward the stove, he noticed Maebry's bedroom door was closed tight, when it had always been open before.

Well, that was another big sign. And it smarted. He sighed, tightening his jaw, and knelt down in front of the wood box. Piece by piece, he stacked the wood inside, quiet so as not to wake her. He had visions of the future, spending nights just like this, being forced to watch while one day some other man courted Maebry and married her. The image made his chest implode, and he winced at the unexpected pain. He was a tough man, but she made him vulnerable. Likely always would.

Although it wasn't his job, had never been in his job description, he went back outside, filled his arms again and carried more wood into the house. Began filling the wood box piece by piece. It would be nice and full come morning for her, so she wouldn't have to step outside in the frigid temperatures before lighting the stove.

Like music, light and sweet and slow, he recognized the gentle tap of her footstep on the stairs. So, guess she wasn't in her room after all. Still, he couldn't look at her. Steeled his spine, kept lowering the last of the chunks of cedar into the bin.

"Gil." Surprise brightened her voice. Not an uneasy tone, as if she were thinking, *great, need to get away from that man.* But a warm tone. As if she didn't mind finding him in her vicinity.

"On a night like this, you should be in the bunkhouse, you know, out of the weather." She padded closer, her skirts rustling. "You do too much for us."

"Can't help myself, since I'm one of the newest hires." He set the last stick of wood down and rose slowly, keeping his voice neutral, friendly. As if that kiss hadn't happened. "You know, I'm still temporary, got to ingratiate myself as much as I can."

"You must like your job."

"Best I've had for the most part." He dusted bits of bark and moss off his gloves, watched it tumble into the wood box, felt her presence like a hot sun at his back. Fighting his feelings for her, larger now and grander, wasn't going to be easy.

"Even with Maureen as your boss?" Politeness was back in her voice. Slightly distant. When he turned around, he could see her reserve, the way she hung in the shadows, staying back from him in the room.

That kiss stood between them in the darkness, like the night.

"Yes, Maureen." He thought of the older lady, crippled and failing. "For the most part, she only yells at me through the window, or if I'm called up to talk with her. I'm tough enough to take a little yelling."

"Still, you don't deserve it. I know all the cowhands think highly of you. You fit in here so well." Maebry wrapped her arms around herself, like a barrier between them.

"How is Maureen doing tonight?" An easier question to ask than the one at the back of his mind, the one he had to get around to asking. Procrastinating a little wouldn't hurt. He crossed his arms over his chest too, a barrier to his heart.

"About the same," Maebry answered politely. "Last I checked, she was sleeping and Aumaleigh was up with her. Keeping the room warm enough is a constant task in this cold."

"And tomorrow is May First. Wonder if the Montgomerys have ever had snow for their annual party?"

"Once, I think, the first year I was here." Maebry shrugged, lowering her arms as if relaxing. "They'll probably have to bring everything indoors, which is too bad because Nora has such beautiful flower gardens. Incredible this time of year, freshly blooming."

"Well, I probably won't mind not seeing that. I'm really not a flower kind of guy." He shrugged.

She smiled. "Really? I'm shocked."

"Figured you might be."

She looked incredible in lamplight. Although she stood at the edges of light, it seemed to find her, reaching out to shine like gold against the sunny highlights in her blond hair. The lamplight cast a golden glow to her ivory complexion. Graced the delicate curve of her face. Nothing could be more captivating. Tenderness rose up from deep within, a tenderness he dared not show.

"Listen, I've got something to say to you and it isn't gonna be easy." He steeled his spine, drawing himself up full height, fisting his hands, doing what had to be done. "About what happened earlier today when I helped you down from the wagon—"

"You mean when you *helped me to the ground?*" She asked pointedly, flushing a bright pink, staring down at the toes of her shoes. "Considering how hard the wind was blowing, it could have knocked me over. I appreciated the help."

"No, that's not what I mean." He steadied his voice, aware of what she was doing. "When I—"

"Hauled the grocery crate out of the wagon for me?" she interrupted, her face turning pinker. "That was considerate of you, too."

"Something tells me you don't want to discuss what really happened." He moved forward, one slow step. Another. A giant shadow, shrinking the size of the kitchen with his masculinity, his magnetic presence. He cleared his throat, his words came quietly, tender. "All I can say is I'm sorry."

"For helping me with my muffler?" She didn't know why tears stood in her eyes. Why it felt like his apology was a rejection. It had to be this way. She just couldn't bear to hear him say the words. "There's nothing to be sorry for."

"I kissed you." His boots knelled softly on the floor, rounding the central work table, coming closer. He took off his hat, held it in his hands. "You avoided me at suppertime, just the way you avoid Lawrence."

"No, it's not like that, Gil." She wanted to cry out, to rush to him, because even in the half-lit room she could see the hurt in his eyes.

The hurt. That realization tore her apart. Never in a million years would she want to hurt Gil. She couldn't stand that he thought that of her. And she couldn't believe that she mattered so much to him. She pointed to the ceiling above. "It was Maureen. She's been in a mood ever since Lawrence came calling. She didn't approve of him asking me to go for a drive."

"So, what did she do to you?" Protectively, his shoulders squared. The angles of his face hardened, his blue eyes darkened.

"Oh, just found some work for me to do."

"That's why you missed supper?" Concern pinched his features, making him somehow more handsome, more desirable. As big and strong as he was, he had a good heart.

That's why she had to fight so hard not to let her feelings for him grow, to keep her heart firmly closed against him. She fisted her hands, when she wanted to reach out to him. She willed her feet to stay in place when she wanted to be closer to him. "I just finished most of the work. Aumaleigh dismissed me, she said I didn't have to finish it. Maureen was asleep and she'd never know."

"That was good of Aumaleigh. I'm glad she looks out for you." He fingered his hat brim, a muscle jumping along his rock-hard jawbone. "Did you get anything to eat?"

"No, I was just going to go to bed."

"Not without a meal, you aren't." He tossed his hat on the work table and reached out for her. When his larger fingers curled around her wrist, snaring her, she tried to ignore the frisson of heat snapping up her arm. She tried to tell herself not to give in, to be strong, but she was weak. She couldn't stop her feet from carrying her along where he directed her. He held out a chair at the small table by the window, the

one she often ate at after the cowboys and Maureen had been served.
"Sit." His command was both firm and mellow. "How many meals have you served me? This time, just this once, let me serve you."

Tears prickled behind her eyes. His kindness would be her undoing. "No, I can't."

"Sorry, I'm not taking no for an answer." His hands moved up her arms, leaving shivery sensations, until they settled on her shoulders. He nudged her downward, into the chair. Unable to resist him, she sat, staring up at him, shadowed and yet more revealed than ever.

Affection brightened the blue shade of his irises, changed and gentled the craggy angles of his face, made him seem ten times more amazing. Her heart rolled over in one unstoppable fall. What was she going to do now?

"I'm not generally this bossy," he explained, moving away from her with measured footsteps, blending into the shadowed corner of the room. A drawer scraped open. "You bring out the worst in me."

"You know I don't like a bossy man." Her voice wobbled, and she fought so hard to keep it from betraying her, from showing feelings she could not confess. "Not at all. Not one bit."

"So I've heard. Guess I'm good and truly out of the running." The edge of a knife refracted the lamplight, then vanished. "Maybe Lawrence really is more your type?"

"Don't even." She rolled her eyes. "Honestly, I did not hear you say that."

"I could help you out by pretending to break up with you tomorrow at the party." There was the thunk of a plate, the scent of fresh bread. "That would free up your path to him."

"Do it and I'll never speak to you again." Now she was smiling, biting her bottom lip, trying not to laugh. The exhaustion she felt slipped away until there was only a glow like the lamplight in the hallway, softly flickering. "Pretend to break up with me, and you become my number one enemy. I'd put you straight to the top of my list."

"You can't fool me. You don't have an enemy list." He turned from the counter, holding a plate in his hand. He emerged from the darkness, a shadow taking on substance, eyes becoming bright blue, those lips that had kissed her cheek saying her name. "Maebry, there is nobody kinder than you."

"Ah, just proves I've been successful in hiding my real self from you." She lifted her chin, determined to fight the pull of him on her soul. She could stay closed to him. "Did you make me a sandwich?"

"Yes, as you've done for me countless times." He set the plate on the table before her. "And for the record, I see you, Sunshine. You're not hiding a thing."

"Not one thing?" Her voice wobbled again, betraying her.

"No." He understood her now, finally had her figured out. Well, at least as much as a man could ever understand a woman. He reached for the pitcher, filled a cup and set it beside her plate. "Tell me why you're still single. How has not one man dropped to his knee at your feet and proposed to you?"

"You know why." Her voice cracked. She stared at the sandwich he'd made, savory stew meat between slices of homemade bread, and didn't reach for it. "I told you. I'm the independent sort. I've decided never to marry. Best to keep control of my life rather than to hand it over to some man who will just tell me what to do."

"Yeah, because that's what marriage is." He pulled out the chair next to her, swung it around and sat down. "That isn't what marriage should be. I know. I watched my uncle treat his wife worse than a rabid coyote that had come into the yard. I also remember my parents. Seemed to me Ma had more of an upper hand than my pa wanted to admit. They were happy."

"That look on your face—" She hesitated, swiped a lock of tumbled down blond hair out of her eyes. "You were a happy little boy."

"I was. Life has a way of surprising you with what happens next, and sometimes what you experience isn't good. But that doesn't diminish the happier times. It only makes them shine brighter. I always figured one day I would meet a lady, I'd let her lasso my heart and we'd be happy together. Just like that."

"Like your parents?" She arched a slender brow, somehow more dear this way, quiet and unguarded. She reached for the glass of water but didn't take a sip. "So what happened with you? Why haven't you found someone who'll marry you?"

"That's a very good question." He watched her take a dainty sip of water, slow deliberate movements, as if she were holding herself very still, waiting for his answer. He shrugged. "I haven't found the one lady who lights up my life."

"Do you really think I'm believing that malarkey?" She arched an eyebrow at him and set down her cup. "My guess is no woman would have you."

"That too. I'm holding out hope, though. Maybe one day a nice lady would come along—"

"Nice?"

"You're right. I'm setting the bar too high. That any woman will come along, old or young, ugly or not, and she won't find me too repulsive—"

"That will be a long shot right there—"

"And since she's desperate with no other prospects, will settle for me as a husband." He feigned a wistful sigh. "It's my dream."

"Be serious." She scowled at him, laughed, shook her head, scattering those wisps of pure gold. "Tell me the truth. I'm curious now."

"I have told you the truth." She had no idea how much it hurt to not be able to say what he felt. "Not about some lady settling for me, but about her lighting up my life. The trouble is, I can only guess she might feel something for me. I don't know because she hasn't said."

"Oh." Maebry bowed her head, the escaped wisps from her braid tumbled forward like a veil, trying to hide her reaction to him. "Maybe she's not free to say something."

"Maybe." His chest twisted, tight and sweet. At least he had his answer for sure. No more guesswork. At least she understood his feelings, so he leaned in, brushed away silken locks of her hair, delicate against his finger, and kissed her cheek. He felt her exhale, as if she'd been holding so much in. She was sweetness itself and he breathed her in, a faint scent of lilacs and lemon oil.

When he pulled away, she didn't move. He sensed sadness, felt it in the stillness between them. He'd go to the ends of the earth, carry the world on his shoulders if he had to, to take away that sadness.

"Guess I'll see you bright and early tomorrow." He climbed to his feet, swung the chair back into place, wishing he had the right to comfort her. To haul her into his arms and profess his intentions to her. But she belonged to another, her life was contractually bound to Maureen. Until that was resolved, he had to be respectful of it. Because when he made a promise to Maebry, it had to be one he could keep.

"For breakfast, right." She tilted her face up, where the lamplight found it. Revealing porcelain-fine cheekbones, the precious curve of her face, the sweep of her long curly lashes. Emotion glinted in her eyes. Was it longing he saw?

"And don't forget you owe me a dance." He wanted to reach for her, lay his hand against the soft side of her face, savor being close to her, maybe press a kiss to her forehead. But he wouldn't do that to her. Not until she was free of her contract. Not until he could show her the dreams he had in store for her.

"Now, eat that sandwich and go to bed." He grabbed his hat, headed away, smiled back at her. Tried to keep the love out of his voice. "Good night, Sunshine."

There were tears in her eyes when he closed the door. The storm hurled ice at him, but he hardly felt it. What he felt inside—the warmth, the light—wasn't something that any storm could dim. Nothing on earth could.

CHAPTER FIVE

He'd called her Sunshine. The honest, undisguised regard and affection in his voice was a sound that stayed with her through her dreams and into the next morning. Every time she thought of it, her chest glowed. But sadness crept in too. It was impossible, but meant the world to know he cared that much for her. Sunshine, he'd called her, the man looking for a woman to light up his life.

A loud *clink* startled her. A fallen spatula, and she must have been the one who dropped it. She blinked, bringing her surroundings into focus and clearing her senses. She stood in front of the cook stove, where bacon sizzled and popped in a frying pan, hashed potatoes browned in a skillet, and a yellow swirl of scrambled eggs were busy congealing in the double skillet. Oops, looked like she'd forgotten to stir them. Imagine the looks on the ranch hands' faces when they saw their breakfast had been ruined. Maybe she'd better pay attention. This was Gil's breakfast too.

"Need any help there?" Josslyn sauntered over with an empty platter. She set it down within easy reach for the eggs, when they were done. "It isn't like you to drop spatulas right and left. If I don't miss my guess, that's an I'm-thinking-of-a-man look you've got on your face."

"I was thinking of the sandwich I had for dinner last night." The one Gil had made her (which had tasted good, by the way). She'd never forget how he'd taken care of her. She tried to wince away the blush on her face, because it was going to give her away. "You know how I love beef sandwiches."

"There it is again. That look." Amused, Josslyn sidled in and stole the spatula. "Move aside. I'm not having this meal ruined by a daydreamer."

"I won't ruin it. I promise to pay better attention." What she didn't want to admit was her feelings for Gil. No, it was better to keep them to herself. If Josslyn knew, then in a blink Aumaleigh and Orla would too. They would root for her, start hoping for her, and that would only feed hopes that could not possibly be met. "Josslyn, let me do my job."

"Sorry, it's almost done anyway. You can flip the bacon for me and drain it." All business, Josslyn expertly stirred the eggs. "I saw your light on pretty late last night. Maureen kept you up again?"

"It wasn't too bad." She grabbed a fork and rescued the smoky bacon slices from the hot pan. The delicious, savory scent of bacon wafted upward, and she breathed it in, making her stomach rumble. "Aumaleigh had it worse. I think she was up most of the night."

"I suspected as much. If the old woman would part with a few of her precious dollars, she could hire help and ease the burden on her daughter." Josslyn's face scrunched up in sympathy for Aumaleigh. "Heaven knows I do all I can to help out, but there aren't enough hours in the day to do it all, not and run this kitchen too. Not that she's paid me last month's wages yet."

"You and everyone else, so I hear." Maebry rescued the last bacon strip and hefted the iron fry pan from the stovetop.

"She's promised to catch everyone up on April's payday," Josslyn's skepticism carried a bite. "Keep in mind, that's today. I didn't see any money for our pay sitting around upstairs yesterday. Did you?"

"No." Maebry swallowed. The ranch's financial management hadn't been handed over to Aumaleigh. No, Maureen kept control, and it was no secret she was behind on her bills. Maebry frowned. The money situation worried her. Her stomach clamped up, sick feeling. What if Maureen kept her threat and sold the contract? It would be a way for the old lady to get cash without digging into her reserves.

Troubled, Maebry popped a cloth over the bacon platter, to keep the meat warm. She hefted the stack of ironware plates off their shelf, and a movement out the window caught her eye. Gil hiking across the yard heading toward the barn. Long-legged stride, confident, striking. All black against the white world. He didn't look her way, he was intent, all business, hat set at a no-nonsense angle, showing only the strong line of his jaw. Remembering his remarkable kiss, she sighed. The warm brush of his lips to her cheek, the tender moment between them, the comfort of his touch. Longing filled her, sweet and strong.

Everything within her ached to go back in time and re-live that one, singular moment again. So she could savor his kiss, memorize every detail. The faint scent of winter on his coat, the clean male scent of his skin, the faint fan of his breath on her cheek—

"Maebry." As if from a great distance, her name was spoken again. "Maebry?"

"Oh!" She blinked, jumped, realized she was staring at Gil as he wrestled open the barn door far across the yard. Realizing she'd been caught staring, heat scorched her face. "Sorry. Daydreaming."

"So I see." Aumaleigh, this time, smiled at her with understanding. She'd entered the room without Maebry noticing, apparently, and had even taken a plate from the stack she held.

Wow, I was really dreaming, she thought, embarrassed. Guess there was no keeping her secret feelings private now.

"As I was saying," Aumaleigh said patiently, her blue gaze softening with what looked like pity. As if she knew exactly how hopeless falling for Gil would be. The older woman stole two slices of bacon from the platter. "I'll bring Mother her breakfast and help out feeding the men. Mother wants you to be on time to the Montgomery's. Leave now, before she starts calling for you. She's in a mood this morning, and I want to spare you that."

"All right." She stared down at her toes, at her patched shoes, one still held on with the twine Gil had given her. "What about you? You were up all night with her again. You have to be exhausted."

"She needed me." Aumaleigh lifted one slender shoulder in a shrug. Weariness marked her face, making her appear almost haggard, her loveliness drained. "I don't think there are many nights left."

"And last I heard the doctor agreed with you," Josslyn spoke up, emptying the scrambled eggs onto the platter. "Tough times, to be sure. Maebry, I'll make up a breakfast sandwich to take with you, but you'd best go get on your coat now. One of the men will take you to town."

"Okay." Resigned, she scurried over to the wall hooks as the conversation silenced. Aumaleigh filled a breakfast plate for her mother, Josslyn rescued biscuits from the oven and popped them into a basket. By the time Maebry finished the last button on her coat, Josslyn was handing her an egg sandwich wrapped in a napkin and waving her out the door.

She crossed the porch, food in hand, wind in her face. While the snow had stopped, the cold had not. The last thing she wanted to do was to work for the Montgomerys, but she had no choice. Maureen had spoken, so she shivered, squinting through the golden glare of dawn toward the barn, waiting for her ride. A man's figure moved across the shadowy open doors of the barn. Gil. He didn't see her, his back was to her as he worked, bending to a cinch, saddling up Casey.

"Hey, there, Maebry!" a friendly voice called out over the squeaking sound of runners on snow, coming from the other direction, surprising her.

She looked up, fighting to keep her gaze from straying toward the open barn doors and Gil, and forced a smile at the young man driving her way. "Hi, Tiernan."

"Guess I'm your driver this morning." He pulled Phil to a stop. "Isn't Josslyn or Orla coming?"

"No, it's just me." Maebry gathered her skirts to climb into the small one-seat sleigh, and Tiernan caught hold of her elbow to help her in. He was only a few years younger than her, just eighteen, but a sweetheart with a sculpted, handsome face, honest, friendly eyes and a smile that had young ladies everywhere swooning and tittering, not that he was aware of it. He felt more like a younger brother to her, just someone to spoil with extra servings of dessert at the supper table.

"How's Maureen?" He held the buffalo robe out for her to take. "Heard the doc was gonna drop by again today."

"Yes, although I'm not sure what more he can do, but it's good of him to try." She settled onto the seat, pulled the buffalo robe over her for warmth and forced her gaze forward on the road ahead, and not behind where she swore she could feel the weight of Gil's stare. Determined, she pressed her lips together, the proper and stoic spinster she needed to be. "Maureen seems worse this morning. According to Aumaleigh, she was having trouble swallowing her morning's tea. Not a good thing."

"I'm sorry." Tiernan snapped the reins. Phil took off with a well-mannered lunge, and the sleigh sped down the hill, runners squeaking against the crisp snow. "Sounds like she's run out of time."

"Yes." Quietly, she settled the robe more snugly around her, bowed her head against the wind, thought of Aumaleigh who'd been up much of the night. Maebry picked at a strand of yarn in her gloves, trying to hide a small hole. She felt sorry for Maureen. Although she had everything—a fine mansion just up the hill behind the trees, one of the biggest and most respected ranches in the country and thought extremely well of herself, Maureen did not appreciate what mattered most. Before her husband had died, their marriage had been as lonely as her widowhood turned out to be. Her sons had scattered, trying to get as far away from her as possible and wanted nothing to do with her. And Aumaleigh, her only daughter, who had managed to love the old woman when no one else could, was treated worse than an indentured servant.

Yes, Maebry thought with pity, Maureen really had nothing at all. At least not the things that mattered.

"So," Tiernan broke into her thoughts, reining Phil through the gate and onto the country road. "You work in the house, you must hear things. Have you heard anything about our pay?"

"You mean, if you're going to get it or not?" Maebry squinted into the bright golden spears of sunlight spiking across the eastern horizon.

"Yep. Everyone's wondering," Tiernan confessed, gloved hands light and easy on the reins. A little sheepish, he shrugged his wide shoulders. "You know, since everyone wasn't paid last month."

"And since this will be your first pay day?" she asked, smiling, feeling lighter now that the ranch and especially Gil was far behind her. If she focused on the beautiful morning, the colorful cloud-strewn sky, the serenity of the sparkling snow in every direction, she could forget her troubles—and almost forget the enormity of what she felt for Gil. "I haven't heard a word."

"Well, this is my first job and I am looking forward to my first pay." Little dimples dug into the corners of his smile. What a cutie. No wonder young ladies giggled whenever he was around. She'd best brace herself, as there'd be plenty of that at the party today. He winked. "Just one of those things that mean I'm my own man."

"That's important with your family." She understood, thinking of

THEN CAME YOU

Tiernan's mother. Nora Montgomery was a force to be reckoned with, not unlike his father. Being from a wealthy family didn't guarantee someone's happiness, anymore than coming from a poor family did, she'd discovered. "Is your father still not speaking to you?"

"Aw, he'll get over it." Tiernan's smile looked a little forced, as if he was hiding his hurt. "He thinks that my taking a job at the ranch is a step down for the family, that there's no future in it."

"I don't know, you could save up your money and buy a ranch one day." She leaned back against the seat as the countryside sped by—snowy trees, the white stretch of meadows, the beleaguered look of cattle pawing through the snow looking for something to eat. In the distance was the dark shadow of town, washed by the golden and pinkish tones of sunrise. She felt calmer here, breathing in the fresh, icy air. "That's how Maureen and her husband made their fortune, okay, along with inheriting more."

He grinned. "See, I've got an inheritance from a great uncle that comes to me when I turn twenty-five. I figure that gives me plenty of time to learn everything I can about running a ranch. When I come into my money, I can buy my own place."

"That sounds perfect to me." She was glad for him, running his own spread, building his life and his future. "You've got a great teacher in Beckett Kincaid. He's the best ranch foreman the Rocking M has ever had."

"Tell me about it." Tiernan's eyes sparkled with excitement, with hope. "I always thought I'd breed and train horses, but I'm getting so much hands-on experience with cattle, and I've learned I like cattle, so that's good right there. I'll figure it out as I go, just like my older brother did."

"Tyler is a great carpenter." She remembered the handsome older Montgomery brother who'd come to repair the barn roof after last summer's storm. He'd talked them into hiring Tiernan when he was through with school. She smiled, liking the way the Montgomery brothers stuck together.

Watching families was a hobby of hers, seeing the good in them, maybe wishing just a little for a family of her own one day. She might be a well-shelved spinster by then, but maybe she still had a chance to marry. Perhaps a widower with children would be looking for a mature bride. She shrugged, a little sad as she thought of Gil. Nine years was too long for him to wait, she knew that. He would figure it out, too. "Tyler is great. Both of my brothers will be at the party today, of course. Father is actually closing the office, so the staff can come too." Tiernan rambled on, talking of his father's unrelenting work ethic, whether his mother was finally going to succeed in setting up his older brother with a bride of her choice, and how much furniture he'd be roped into moving for his mother, who would no doubt be in a state due to the snow in her prized flower gardens.

Maebry listened, nodding at the appropriate times, but part of her mind drifted. Where did it go? Right back to Gil. Last night, standing half in shadow, half in light, he'd made a sandwich and served it to her. And those things he'd said to her…why, her eyes teared, remembering. He'd made her feel special and important to him. Loved.

It was a feeling she never wanted to forget.

* * *

Aumaleigh McPhee pushed straggling hair out of her eyes, ignored the weariness bearing down on her like a speeding freight train and winced as her tired back protested in pain. She reached for a fresh clean nightgown, bunched the soft flannel up in her hands and gently slid it over her mother's head. Maureen, too exhausted by pain, could not lift off the pillow, so Aumaleigh did it for her, cupping the back of her head gently and tugged down the thickness of the material until it rested on her mother's wasted, skeletal shoulders.

"You pulled my hair. You're just worthless." Maureen snapped, pruning her face, although only the left side moved. "I don't know why I had you, you are a bane to my existence. A waste, that's what you are."

With forbearance, Aumaleigh gritted her teeth, determined not to let her temper rise. That was what Mother wanted. "Remember what the doctor said? You're to stay calm and rest. You must stay very calm. He thinks you had a small stroke last night."

"That doctor." One side of Maureen's mouth curled up with a snarl. "There's an imbecile if I ever saw one. Who does he think he is, that's what I want to know? Strutting in here as if he's a gift to the world, lying. That's what he's doing. I'm not dying. This sickness is all because of him. It's his doing, that medicine he wants me to take. I'm not taking it anymore. I'm too smart for that."

"All right." Aumaleigh knew better than to argue, for that would only escalate Mother's behavior. With a sigh, she shook out the nightgown's long sleeve and reached for her mother's withered arm.

"Don't insult me, you stupid girl." Maureen jerked up her good arm, although she had little control of it. "I can do this myself. Why I have to put up with you, I don't know."

Hard to know what to say to that. Aumaleigh's jaw strained, her chest felt ready to explode from everything she held inside. For fifty two years, she'd been Maureen's daughter and was well used to her treatment, even if it hurt. Surely she could take it a little bit longer.

She held the nightgown's sleeve as Maureen attempted to stab her hand into the arm hole, time and time again. Finally, she succeeded. Sweat dotted the old woman's forehead and she'd turned gray from the effort.

At least now she'd likely be quiet while Aumaleigh finished dressing her. Making sure the sleeve was in place, there was no fabric wrinkled or bunched to cause discomfort, she reached across, lifted her mother's paralyzed left arm and fitted it into the sleeve. Gently peeled the covers back, bit by bit, she eased the fabric down over her mother's wasted body, easing her gently forward when necessary, lifting her up until the warm flannel draped her completely.

"Now the warm pair of slippers Maebry knitted for you." Aumaleigh fetched them from the nightstand, soft, thick wool in tiny, perfect stitches to keep in the heat. She sat on the edge of the bed. "These will keep you toasty. By the feel of things, I need to put more wood on the fire."

"Maebry should have built it up before she left. That lazy girl, I know you let her go to bed last night. And with her work unfinished!" Maureen had developed a slur, but that didn't lessen the bite to her words. "And if she thinks she can charm a man into marrying her and paying off her contract, she'd better think again. She's my servant."

"Why shouldn't Maebry find love?" Aumaleigh fought down anger. Failed. Probably because it was an old issue, one that hurt too much to think about. She turned her back to her mother, scrunched up the knit slipper she held and wedged it onto Maureen's gnarled and bloodless foot.

But the memories came up anyway, images of a tall, strapping man with a rumbling baritone—even in memory and after all these years the sound made her melt. She squeezed her eyes shut, growing still for a moment, keeping the memory inside...and the pain.

"Maebry belongs to me, that's why!" Mother huffed, struggling as a breathing fit took her over. She wheezed, grew red, but that didn't stop her tirade. "I bought her fair and square, I own her, and she'll serve her term or else."

Hard to know how to answer that. Especially since the doctor had been clear, any upset could trigger another stroke. Aumaleigh shook her head, tugged too hard on the slipper and left it slightly askew on Mother's foot. A hot, hard ball of outrage expanded in the pit of her stomach, growing larger and larger with every breath. Well, when she inherited, she would be in charge of Maebry's contract. The first thing she'd do was to give Maebry her freedom. And then she and Gil could move forward with their relationship.

The image of that—of Gil taking Maebry by the hand and courting her properly, one day kneeling down to ask her to be his wife, of the happiness they would share, of the family they would have—made tears burn in her eyes. Aumaleigh pushed off the bed, stopped to draw up the quilt over her mother's wasted form and whipped around, pounding across the room.

The sound of another's footsteps startled her. She glanced over her shoulder, nearly stumbling when she recognized the town lawyer. Amiable Nate Denby hesitated outside the bedroom door, a bundle of papers tucked in the crook of one arm, a tousled lock of brown hair tumbling over his forehead. In his early thirties, he had kind eyes, spectacles and the kind of bookish-handsomeness that was very nice.

"Aumaleigh." His smile widened, showing hints of dimples. "Josslyn said to come on up. I have an appointment with your mother."

"If she's up to it." The decades of unhappiness being her mother's caretaker warred with the love of her mother, as it always did. The daughter in her yearned for a mother's love, as it always would. She glanced at the cadaverous woman on the bed with her chin touching her chest and her eyes closed. Being bathed and freshly dressed had been a strain. Aumaleigh shrugged. "Looks like she's napping. Would you like me to fix you a cup of coffee, maybe warm up a cinnamon roll for you? You can wait downstairs?"

"I'd like that."

"Good. I don't think she'll be asleep for long."

"That's fine. I don't mind waiting a bit." Nate's friendly gaze radiated warmth. She liked his easy going manner, and that relaxed manner reminded her of the man she'd fallen in love with decades ago.

Although her Gabriel had been a cowboy, strapping and strong. She gasped as the memory stole over her, she could not stop it. In her mind's eye, she saw Gabriel, Stetson tilted to shadow his face, giving light only to his strong, square jaw and whisker stubble. Her fingers tingled, remembering just how it felt to run her fingertips along that iron jaw line.

Enough, Aumaleigh, she told herself, kneeling to set a fresh piece of wood onto the grate. It tore out her heart to remember, and she had enough heartbreak now to deal with. She suspected the doctor, when he arrived shortly, would have even more bad news for her.

Sadly, she brushed bark and moss off her hands, watched the fire claim the new chunk of log, and flames snapped and popped, warming the room.

"Nathaniel Denby?" Mother croaked, opening one eye. "Is that you standing there, about to leave?"

"Well, I was only going downstairs, Maureen." Nate tossed Aumaleigh a helpless look, patient, as always, with her mother.

"Well, think again." Mother scowled, as much as her slack face would allow. "Get over here. We have business and it doesn't involve anyone else. Aumaleigh, get your big behind out of here and close the door behind you. Stop dragging your feet."

Aumaleigh sighed, remembering a time when Mother's hurtful and inaccurate comments had been hard to take as a young girl growing up. She slipped past Nate, offered him a sympathetic look because doing business with Maureen was never easy, stepped into the small hallway and closed the door tight. Hard to explain the jumble of emotions tangled up inside her, although they made it hard to breathe. Her ribs ached as if they were broken.

Heaven knew love wasn't always easy and families could be complicated. But as time went by and her mother's condition worsened, she'd hoped for some kind of reconciliation. For a chance to repair the hurts of a lifetime and be able to see the good in Mother. To laugh with her, to share with her, to make some kind of a loving bond before it was too late.

She knew now that was never going to happen. Heart heavy, she took two steps and spotted someone else in the kitchen. Gil Blackburn.

Her breath caught, and she gripped the banister tightly, knowing without words why he was here.

He'd come to ask Maureen if he could buy out Maebry's contract. Aumaleigh hung her head, hesitating in the middle of the stairs. She already knew how that was going to go.

CHAPTER SIX

"The Missus is coming." A dapper butler, sporting gray hair and wearing a perfectly pressed suit, popped into the kitchen doorway, holding the swinging door open with a narrow shoulder. "Just thought you might need warning. She's on a rampage, but you didn't hear it from me."

"It's the snow." The Montgomery's cook stirred something steaming in a pot, ruddy from the heat. The pleasant woman shook her head, as if in disapproval. "Having to move the party inside is messin' up her plans. A lot of good it'll do to punish us all for it."

"I agree, but you didn't hear that from me either." Harvey the butler winked, let the door swing shut and left the army of workers in the kitchen to their frenzied tasks.

Maebry finished scraping one carrot and grabbed for another. Off the peelings went, tumbling onto the counter. The back of her neck ached from the nonstop work—she'd been on carrot duty now for almost an hour—and still had a ways to go. How many carrots did one party need?

"My arm is about ready to fall off," Missy, the blond kitchen maid standing next to her, commented ruefully, stopping to rub her shoulder. A mini-mountain of denuded potatoes sat beside her. Missy reached for a potato from the sack and immediately started peeling. "This must be a really big party. I just moved here, so I've never seen one of the

Montgomery parties."

"I have." Maebry couldn't help the note of wistfulness creeping into her words. Probably because she thought of last year's party, when there had been no Gil. Of course, no other man had caught her eye, but the local schoolteacher, Sarah Combs, had been surrounded by all the eligible bachelors in town (and there were many since there was a surplus of men and a shortage of marriage-aged women). "They are lovely. Everyone who is anyone in the county attends."

"I heard a real string quartet will be playing." Missy sighed as she bowed her head, rotating the potato in her palm as she peeled, knife flashing. "I've never heard of such a thing. I grew up on a Minnesota farm."

"I grew up on a farm, too." Although she'd eventually gotten used to being surrounded by luxury serving in the McPhee Manor house, before the damaging storm. "When I came to work for Maureen, it was like serving for the Queen of England. That's how fancy it was—"

She fell silent as the kitchen doors swung open again and a regal, handsome woman sashayed in, draped in a flawless ruby-colored gown. Her blond hair was so light, it shone platinum in the sunlight streaming through the many windows. Her face carried middle-aged hints of a greater beauty she must have had in her prime. Her gaze narrowed as she scanned the room. She zeroed in on Maebry. "You, there. Come with me."

Maebry gulped, set down her knife, felt Missy's silent sympathy as she stepped away. Her hands were stained orange from the carrot peeling, so she swiped them the best she could on her apron. From years with Maureen, she was afraid to address Mrs. Montgomery, although she wondered what the woman wanted. Surely it was too much to hope she would be sent home, no longer needed.

"The stable boy and driver are not making adequate progress with the snow shoveling." The fine lady waltzed down the hallway, through an exquisite dining room where a pair of maids were setting out linens and china, and heading in the direction of the front door. Quality and elegance were everywhere—the graceful line of an imported sofa, the arches of the intimately coved ceilings, the glint off the tasteful crystal chandeliers. Mrs. Montgomery frowned at her. "You look sturdy enough, and I can't count all the times Maureen has told me you can work like a horse and not feel it. Work is what you're good for."

Mrs. Montgomery paused, looked Maebry up and down and frowned again, as if unsure of that statement. Maebry stared at her shoes, feeling inadequate, feeling every inch of her shabby clothes and her station in life.

"Go on with you now. Don't stop until the work is done." The regal lady gestured with a wave of one soft hand in the direction of the entrance.

She bobbed the required curtsey at the lofty Mrs. Montgomery. Sure enough, a shovel was waiting for her, leaning against the wall by the front door.

Woodenly, she went in search of her coat and returned, buttoned up and ready to face the chill. The late morning sun angled across the yard, casting small shadows on decorative trees and precious bushes and flowers mantled by a foot and a half of white. The rhythmic scrapes of shovels against bricks drown out the usual sounds of wind and merry birds.

An older man looked up from his shoveling, his forehead furrowing as if puzzled. "I asked the Missus for another hand, and she sends you? You're just a bit of a thing."

"But I'm strong." She didn't mention all the times she'd filled in at the barn, mucking out stall after stall. Very physical work. It wasn't much different here. "Where would you like me?"

"Inside, with the other maids." The man shook his head, giving her a sympathetic look. "But I suppose that won't go over with the Missus. Better clear the stairs, then, and the porch. That's the lightest work I have out here."

"Thank you, sir." Relieved at his kindness, she gripped the shovel's handle tightly, sized up the problems of the drifted snow on the porch, and got to work.

As she scooped up her first shovel full of white stuff, she heard the clomp of a horse in the drive and the squeak of sled runners on the snow. Something clicked in her heart, like a key turning in a lock, opening that door within, the one needing to stay closed. If she was going to fight her feelings for Gil, that is.

She didn't need to turn around to know who'd arrived. She felt his nearness as surely as the porch boards at her feet. His presence seemed to fill her like a new sun, threatening to light up the dark. Tender emotions she had to resist flickered to life, affection and caring that

57

could never be expressed or realized. She tossed a load of the snow over the rail and hunkered down for another shovelful.

"Casey, you nut." Gil's voice drifted on the wind. "Go with Agnew. He's got grain. Yeah, I thought you'd like that."

"He's a handsome fellow," a man's voice answered, presumably Agnew. A set of boots and horse hooves sounded in the snow, traveling around the far side of the house.

The silence she felt within as she waited for Gil to come closer ached like an old wound. Maebry stiffened, fighting the pull of him on her heart, both dreading the moment when she looked up into his familiar gaze and wanting it so much. Needing to see him, hungering for the sight of his smile, the feel of his substantial, dependable presence. The spot on her forehead tingled in memory of his last kiss, the one that had felt like resignation. How could she look at him the same now, when they couldn't be together?

His boots crunched in the snow. His voice rumbled low and deep, friendly, as he chatted with one of the other shovelers. Maebry dumped a load of snow over the porch railing, feeling the icy wind and the heat of his gaze. She didn't want to look at him. She didn't think she could bear to.

Her spine shivered at the knell of his footsteps coming closer. Up the steps, across the porch. She stiffened, scooped up a shovelful of snow and swung away from him, sending it flying over the banister into the yard. It would be easier if he kept on walking, went inside without stopping to say hello. She didn't know where they went from here. She saw only her breaking heart. Gil was simply so easy to love, and she cared more than she could admit.

Far too much.

"Maebry." His words warmed the air, drove the chill from the wind, made the sun brighter. "Give me that shovel. You shouldn't be out here doing a man's work."

"I don't mind." She hoped her forced smile would fool him. She spun toward him, pretending seeing him didn't break her apart. Oh, how good he looked standing there, limned by sunlight, substantial and masculine, dressed all in black. She ignored the squeeze of her chest, the kick of her pulse and the wishes rising. "I'll take working out in the fresh air any day so thanks, but I'll be keeping this shovel. What are you doing here? You've not come to do work, I bet."

"I will be lending a hand with the horses. In weather like this, they'll need to be blanketed and stabled." Gil's knowing gaze searched hers, as if he wasn't fooled. "Not that I'm here of my own free will. Maureen ordered it when I spoke to her today."

"You spoke to her about the ranch?" She scrunched up her forehead, wondering why. "Beckett's usually the one who has to deal with her. Let me think...it's not his day off."

"No, I needed to talk to her about a different matter." He lowered his voice, wrapped his large hands around the shovel handle and tugged until he pulled it from her grip.

She wanted to protest but he leaned in, his big body blocking the wind and sun until all she could see was him. The midnight blue flecks in his blue irises, the caring reflected there, the importance of what he was about to say. Easy to read the sadness in those bright blue depths, feel the weight of it in the air between them. His gloved hand brushed the curve of her face, as tenderly as a dream.

"I asked Maureen if I could buy out your contract." He spoke quietly, so his words wouldn't carry, holding all the weight of his disappointment.

"You *what?*" Her jaw dropped. Shock catapulted through her. Surely she'd heard him wrong. *"What did you do?"*

"I asked to buy your freedom."

"No. Tell me, you didn't." Panic jolted through her, so hard it rattled her teeth. She stared up at him, aghast, horrified. "Gil! Why would you do such a thing?"

"Because it's what I want for you." His square jaw tensed, muscles bunching along the jawbone. The tenderness in his blue gaze disappeared, becoming shadowed with hurt. "I didn't think you'd react like this."

"Clearly." She opened her mouth to say more, didn't know what on earth to say or where to start, so she pressed her hands to her face, felt the icy wool from her gloves against her cheeks, unworthy. She did not deserve this, it was too much to ask of the man she cared about. No, *cared about* was too small of a word for what she felt for her Gil. She felt as if her ribs were cracking too, spearing every internal organ. It took all her strength to pull her hands from her face, fighting down her emotions, and meet his troubled gaze.

"I thought it would make you happy, that we could be together."

Gil looked struck. His chiseled mouth swooped downward in the corners. Pain clouded his honest eyes. "I don't understand. I thought you cared about me. I thought—" He hesitated, as if he were about to say something, perhaps bare his heart, but changed his mind.

Great, now she'd gone and hurt him. She gritted her teeth, felt a deep rending in her heart. "You can't have had the time to save up that kind of money, Gil, which means you'd be the one in debt to Maureen. No, that's too much of a sacrifice. It's not what I would ever want for you."

"I see." He said the words slowly, digesting them. Tendons corded in his neck as he thought things over. "Last night, I thought I made it clear how I felt."

"You did." Tears stood in her eyes. She blinked, as if fighting to control them. Her lovely face crinkled up unhappily, leaving so much unspoken. "It's simply too much money, Gil. You need to talk to Maureen and take back your offer. Otherwise, I won't be able to live with myself."

"I see." He rocked back on his heels, drew in a breath, let her words settle. That was Maebry, thinking of everyone before herself. He should have known. It only made him love her more. "Well, no worries. She said no."

"Oh, that doesn't really surprise me," Maebry said with a wry twist of a smile and a shrug of her slender shoulders. She looked small and vulnerable in her worn old coat and fraying mittens. "It would be a lot of trouble to find another indentured servant."

"Right." The pain of his failure tore through him. He wanted to save her. He wanted to give her a better life, to make sure she was happy, his precious Maebry. The sadness wreathing her dear face tore him apart.

Footsteps sounded on the steps behind him before he could draw her close. He glanced over his shoulder, grimaced at the sight of Agnew waiting for him.

"Gil, I could use some help." The older gentleman hiked up a bushy silver eyebrow. "The first of the guests are starting up the drive."

"Fine, I'll be right there." Wishing he could be everything Maebry needed, Gil retrieved the shovel and held it out to her, sorry he had no spare time to clear the porch for her. He felt like he was breaking apart when he took that first step away from her.

"This isn't over," he warned her gently, because he'd figured out why she was so upset.

The tears in her eyes brimmed, rolling down her cheeks.

"It has to be." She took the shovel and turned away from him.

No, he didn't want to accept that. He couldn't let this be over. She meant too much to him. Nothing hurt worse than walking away from her, fearing she was right. That their love was never meant to be.

* * *

Gil was not going to waste his life's savings on her, and that was that, or spend even one second working off a debt for years to come. No way, no how. It was too much of a sacrifice. Maebry thunked down the bowl next to the undecorated layer cake sitting on the Montgomery's kitchen counter. He'd worked too hard for his savings. He deserved his dreams, the very best future, which he would not have if he mortgaged it for her.

No, she didn't want that for him. Which meant she would have to let him go. Her heart cracked apart at the thought. She reached for a clean spatula, blinking her blurry eyes. Concentrate on your work, Maebry, she told herself, focusing on the drone of the women's voices surrounding her, rising and falling as they scurried here and there in the crowded kitchen, frantic to finish their tasks. On the wall overhead, the clock ticked down the hour.

"We've got twelve minutes!" Cook armed herself with oven mitts and banged open the door. "Missy, are the potatoes done? Check them for me, dear. Lucile, did you fetch the cream from the cellar?"

Answers shouted out above the chaos, and Maebry tuned them out, dipped the spatula in the freshly whipped frosting and turned toward the cake. Her hand shook as she remembered the hurt and then the determination on Gil's sculpted face. The pinch of his mouth, the jut of his granite chin, the muscles bunching along his rock-hard jaw. He didn't look like a man who would let this go.

"Good job." Lucile, second in command in the kitchen bopped over to inspect Maebry's work. "You have a flare. Be sure and layer it thickly. The Missus is particular about her cakes."

"I'll do my best," she promised, plopping a dollop of frosting on top and spreading it around. Lucile rushed off, leaving her alone, and her gaze drifted to the window. She could see a distant corner of the barn, but not Gil, and she gave a troubled sigh. *This isn't over*, he'd said.

Then she would have to end it. Because she loved him. She'd cut all ties to him, never speak to him again. That would do it. Satisfied, she swirled frosting, scrunching her face up in thought. It would make things awfully uncomfortable around the ranch. Imagine darting through doorways and lingering in empty rooms just to avoid him. But come mealtime, there would be no dodging him. When she set out the platters of food on the dinner table, she'd simply have to do her best to ignore him.

Pain serrated her heart. She rubbed the heel of her hand against her sternum. Just think of her life without Gil in it—there would be no friendship, no laughter, no conversations between them. Just distance and uneasiness. She bit her bottom lip, deeply miserable. See what a mistake it had been to let her feelings get out of control? Now they were impossible to reel back in. Why had she done it?

Because she'd been weak, unable to control her heart. She'd known all along she couldn't marry him, but now they couldn't even be friends. That loss struck hard, and she swallowed down the sob rising in her throat. Focusing on the last glop of frosting in the bowl, she swirled it onto her spatula and gave the cake a finishing touch.

"It's time!" Cook clapped her hands above the frenetic noise in the kitchen. Chatter silenced, knives stilled, the staff paraded by the counters and like a well-disciplined army lifted platters and bowls, steaming with delicious food. "Lucile, you lead. Missy, get in the back. Don't spill a drop of that gravy. Maebry, carry the bowls of string beans and carrots, that's a love."

Ready to help, she nodded in agreement, set aside the spatula and snatched up the designated bowls. Carrots in a butter glaze steamed up at her, emitted a delicious aroma, although when she breathed in the green beans with crumbled bacon, her stomach rumbled hungrily. Who wouldn't salivate, she thought as she slipped into the back of the line of servers. This was a feast fit for royalty.

"I can't believe all this food," Missy turned around in line to whisper, then fell silent when Cook gave her a squinty eye. Deportment mattered in the Montgomery household.

Maebry squared her shoulders, straightened her spine and did her best to look presentable as she paraded past Cook, through the doors and into the hallway. The conversations of the awaiting guests echoed in the coved ceiling overhead, and the beams of golden light from the chandeliers cast a heavenly glow over the luxurious room.

Fine furniture gleamed, crystal glittered, real silver glinted in the light. The best linen money could buy draped the main dining table and several that had been brought in from other rooms. The seated guests all turned to comment in anticipation of the delicious food. Maebry kept her eyes on the ground, careful not to tread on the backs of Missy's shoes, feeling anonymous in her black maid's dress and white ruffled apron, borrowed from the uniform closet. The skirt was a tad shorter than she'd hoped, showing the upper portion of her shoe. She hoped no one noticed the twine holding it onto her foot. . . .

No one seemed to. Only one man watched her with a steady, claiming gaze. Gil shifted in his chair as she circled toward him. He stopped in mid-sentence, ignoring one of the Montgomery brothers he'd been speaking with. The corners of his mouth upturned, the intensity shadowing his bright blue eyes darkened. The noise in the room silenced, everything faded away as if it were only the two of them. Her breathing stilled, she wasn't even sure if her heart was beating as Gil's gaze sank into hers. Her skin tingled as she swept past him. Every hair on her arm stood at attention. Aware of him. Affected by him.

"It's a shame Aumaleigh couldn't be here." A woman's voice came as if from a great distance. "The rumors about Maureen must be true. How is she doing, Maebry?"

At the sound of her name she blinked, breaking the hold Gil had on her. The room around her rushed in—the bright lamplight, the many tables ringing with conversation, the guests merry. She set down the bowls of vegetables on the table next to Sarah Combs's dinner plate. The young woman, who was the local schoolteacher, looked up at her expectantly, auburn-brown curls framing her pretty face.

"Uh, Maureen is struggling." She kept her voice low, so it wouldn't carry. No doubt Mrs. Montgomery would not approve of her servants speaking with the guests. "We fear she had a small stroke last night, so Aumaleigh didn't want to leave her side."

"Understandable." Sarah nodded in sympathy. "I'll try and stop by and see Aumaleigh. Maybe relieve her for a bit so she can get a little rest. I imagine you've tried."

"Yes, but she refuses to budge." Maebry bit her lip, fighting sadness on so many levels. "The doctor says it won't be long now. In the meantime, I worry about Aumaleigh's health."

"You're a good friend to her." Sarah patted Maebry's arm, a kind touch, meant to comfort. "You look like you've been carrying a hard workload too. I—"

A sharp, scolding sound interrupted. Mrs. Montgomery cleared her throat, sending a pointed look Maebry's way. Caught, Maebry bowed her head, backed away, heart pounding. As she retraced her steps, hurrying to catch up with the other departing maids, she snared Gil's gaze. The arch of his brows, the tender look on his face, the determination in the set of his jaw. What was she going to do about that?

"Save a dance for me, Sunshine," he murmured as she swept by.

She squeezed her eyes shut, weak for just an instant, and kept on going. Why did he have to be so wonderful? It made it so much harder to do the right thing, to let him go. Tears blurred her vision, but she blinked them away. She cared about Gil far too much to let him sacrifice his future for her. Then he would be the one indebted to Maureen or to her heirs (she knew for a fact Aumaleigh would not inherit, as everyone expected).

Frustrated, miserable and hurting, she scurried into the kitchen to help with the clean up. At least kitchen work would keep her safe from Gil and out of his sight. Too bad it wouldn't keep him out of her heart.

CHAPTER SEVEN

"**M**aebry!" Cook shouted over the clanging of pans and chiming of plates as the last of the dishes were being washed and put away by the army of workers. "Someone to see you."

It wasn't Gil. She knew that by the silence in her heart. Thank goodness. She set down her dishtowel, peered around Missy who was on tiptoe wrestling a big kettle back onto the overhead shelf, and spied a dapper-looking fellow in the doorway, minus his bowler hat.

She groaned. Not Lawrence Latimer.

"Go on with you, now. We're almost done here." Cook went back to scrubbing the stove. "Have some fun, love."

"Oh." Not sure that being with Lawrence qualified as fun, Maebry thought. It seemed there was no escape. Where was a fake beau when you needed one? And why did Gil have to go and be so wonderful? She stumbled forward, taking small steps to prolong the moment.

"You grow lovelier by the day, my dear Maebry." Lawrence threw back his inadequate shoulders, puffed up his thin chest. He wasn't the handsomest fellow, but his eyes flashed kindness as he held out one soft hand to take hers.

"You flatter me too much, I'm afraid." Uncomfortable with his compliments and his attention, she blushed. "I'm average at best. You're very kind, Lawrence."

"I'm hoping that's an attribute you might value in a suitor?" He quirked an eyebrow as he reached out to take possession of her hand. His touch was cool, impersonal. "I noticed Gil left the party a bit ago."

"Oh." She swallowed, wondering why he'd left. Because she'd tried to reject him or because something was wrong at the Rocking M? She thought of Maureen's frailness and her stomach cramped. She stared down at the toes of her shoes, telling herself it didn't matter. Gil had left. At least she wouldn't have to worry about him tracking her down for a dance, the way Lawrence obviously had.

She tried to tug free her hand from Lawrence's rather damp grip, but he had a death hold on it and it took some tugging. "I'm not serious with Gil either. I can't be. I owe Maureen too much money, and I could never in good conscience allow you or anyone else to pay my debt."

"But if I marry you, then it would become *my* debt, not yours." Lawrence opened the back door for her, a courteous gentleman. She lead him out onto the porch where the sun shone bright and snow melted from the roof and nearby trees with a cheerful, melodic *drip-drop, drip-drop*.

"You are a good man, Lawrence." She hated being the reason for the disappointment creasing across his face. Gently, so she would not hurt his feelings any further, she said what she'd been trying to avoid. But there was no other choice now than to be honest.

"I don't care about you in that way." She met his gaze directly, so he would know she meant every word. "Somewhere in this world there is the perfect lady for you. When you find her, you'll know. You'll be able to look into her eyes and see a lost piece of your soul. You'll know what she is about to say before she says it. When your hands touch, it's like your hearts are joined together, beating as one. That's what you deserve, Lawrence. It's what I'll be wishing for you."

He cleared his throat, stared down at the floor for a moment, gave a little shrug. When he met her gaze, his smile was bittersweet. "That's the nicest rejection I've ever had."

"Well, I am sorry for it." She felt tingles shiver down her spine. Every nerve ending in her skin flickered. That could only mean one thing. She waited until Lawrence had retreated back into the house and closed the door before she turned around, already knowing who had returned to the party.

Gil stood on the porch step, hands on his hips, watching her. His eyes shone darkly, as if with mystery. The line of his jaw looked rigid, uncompromising. Feelings she could not hold back rushed forward, affection too great to be confined.

"I heard what you said about finding the right person." His baritone rumbled through her as if his words were her own. His breath, his heartbeat moved hers. When he towered over her, he seemed to suck the oxygen from the air. She couldn't breathe, not unless he did. A corner of his mouth quirked upward. "You were talking about us, weren't you?"

"No," she lied, because she had to protect him. She had to do right by him. This was Gil, wonderful Gil.

When the palm of his hand pressed against the curve of her face, his touch was more than flesh to flesh, skin to skin. She felt his soul in that touch. They stood in silence, and she sensed realization move through him, silently understanding everything.

Just everything.

"You cannot push me away. You cannot scare me away." He drew her against him, into the amazing invincible wall of his chest. "You can't force me away. No matter what, I'm not going anywhere. I love you, Maebry."

"I don't want you to." She burrowed against him, heaven knew she could not help herself. Pain prickled behind her eyelids and scorched her heart. "I won't let you sacrifice so much for me."

"I wish you would." He folded his strong arms around her, bringing her snugly against him. Tenderness resonated in his words. "It would be done out of great affection."

"Oh, Gil." She squeezed her eyes shut, holding back the burst of joy, the explosion of hope at his words, hope and joy she didn't want to feel. This wasn't what she wanted, to be a burden to him. She buried her face in his coat, at a loss. "I told you no. You'll be throwing away your future."

"What's my future without you?" He rested his chin on the top of her head, breathing her in. "I worked hard all these years because I want a better life. I want a dream. Now you're that dream."

"No." She wanted to pull back, wanted to say anything to make him change his mind, but his words touched her soul. It still didn't make it right. "It is too high of a price to pay. Believe me, I know what it's like to be trapped, when your life isn't really your own."

"I don't mind." He didn't even blink. So stalwart, so loyal and true.

"But I do." She pushed away from him, hating the way his arms fell away from her, hating the cold air rushing over her, where his body had warmed hers. Anguish tore through her. "I'm not worth it."

"You're worth everything." Unyielding love flashed in his blue eyes. Easy to see the strength of that would never fade. "Maureen isn't long for this world, the doctor said she has days at best. And while I'm sorry for that, may her passing be an easy one, I intend to make an offer to her heir. Then you'll be free to let me court you the right way. Free to marry me when the time is right."

"Oh, Gil." The burn behind her eyes became unbearable, but it was nothing compared to the agony in her heart. The agony from his kindness, from his love. She smiled through her tears. Why couldn't she resist teasing him? "Well, what if when I'm free, I don't want you to court me?"

"Then I'm in big trouble." He moved in, took her hands in his. Big, strong, male-hot. In that instant, with his sweet touch, her heart belonged to him, no longer hers. The corners of his mouth quirked upward into a mischievous grin. "Don't tell me after all this that I might lose out to Lawrence?"

"It's a close one, a real tough choice. Right now I can't say how this will turn out." Sure, she was joking, but only to hide what he meant to her. The depth of his love for her, for his sacrifice for her, it just blew her away. "You know I have nothing to give you, Gil. Not like what you've given me."

"Oh, yes you do." He tugged her against him, wrapped her in his arms, gazed down at her with infinite affection. She could read forever in his eyes, forever and a day. He smiled, slanting his lips over hers. "I'll settle for your love. Sunshine, you are worth anything, any sacrifice I have to make."

As if to prove it, his lips grazed hers, settled in and claimed. She placed her hands along his powerful jaw, felt the faint texture of his skin and whiskers, felt the punch of guilt in her heart. The firm, velvet-soft caress of his kiss sizzled along her lips and she clung to him, barely able to breathe, unable to move, mesmerized by the sensation of her heart coming alive in ways it had never been before. Of the depth of commitment she felt, the devotion knitting into her soul.

When he lifted his lips from hers, they stood in silence gazing into each other's eyes, surrounded by sunlight as spring returned to the world around them. She drew in a slow breath, never wanting this moment to end.

"Come here, Sunshine." He pulled her snug against him, folding her against his powerful chest. "I just want to hold you."

"I know the feeling." She sighed, burrowing into him, never wanting to let him go. Nothing was sweeter than being in his arms, her cheek pressed against his coat, listening to the reliable thump of his heart. Yes, this is how she wanted to spend forever.

Not that it was possible, so she held him while she could. Holding on, when she should be letting go.

* * *

Aumaleigh took the empty tea cup from Doc Hartwell and carried it over to the wash basin. Those few steps gave her a moment to compose herself. One look at the physician's weathered face told her exactly what she feared. Not a surprise, as this day had been a long time coming, Mother had been suffering from her wasting disease for two decades now, but still. It would be hard to take. She set the saucer down with a clink, took a moment to breathe in the silence of the still house, fortified herself with as much strength as she could.

"You were right to have me come and check her again. Often small strokes are a precursor to something worse." The doc's boots knelled slowly on the hardwood, coming closer. Voice low, so his words wouldn't carry upstairs where Mother lay resting. The older gentleman's face wreathed in compassion. "You must prepare for the end, I'm afraid. I wish I had better news."

"Me, too. Mother has fought so hard for so long." Her throat choked closed, cutting off her words. A surge of raw, horrible grief rolled up, flooding her chest, driving out every other feeling. It didn't matter that her mother had been impossible to deal with, she still loved the woman—the woman who had cost her so much. She closed her eyes against the hot seep of tears. Now was not the time to give into them. She held herself upright, grabbing the counter for support. "What can I do for her?"

"Just keep her comfortable and very calm. I know that's hard with Maureen, but this is important. I've left more laudanum on the corner of the table there." Doc's tone softened. "You are working too hard,

Aumaleigh, caring for her. Perhaps you can hire someone to help for this last little bit. You mustn't wear down your health."

"That's good advice, thank you." She wearily shook her head, Mother had been worse than ever about holding onto money and to the control of it. Refusing to delegate, refusing to accept her coming death. There would be no extra money in the household budget she gave them to pay for a helper. Weary, she pushed away from the counter. "What should I watch for, so I know when to call for you next?"

"It could go very fast, be over in a moment." The doc frowned, buttoned his coat, his deep tenor layered with sadness. It must be hard to give this kind of sad news. "Or she could linger for a few more days. She's having difficulty breathing, and her heartbeat is irregular. Those are signs the end is near. You call me anytime you want to, Aumaleigh. You don't question it, you just send one of your men riding for me, even if it's in the wee hours of the night."

Kindness. Aumaleigh winced, doing her best to hold back her emotions. She appreciated the doc more than he knew. "Thank you for coming. I know you're missing the Montgomery's party."

"Truth is, I don't much mind." Doc winked, heading toward the door, medical bag in hand. "You know I like to play my fiddle for the social events in this town, but I don't always get along with Nora. If it was one of her son's birthdays or something, I'd be there. But as it is, I'm happier working. Are you sure you don't need anything else?"

"I'm good, Doc." She saw him to the door, held it open as he ambled through, gave him a wave as he strode across the porch. Melting snow tinkled and chimed, merry as a melody while the sun blazed with a summer's heat. Crazy weather. She shook her head, closed the door and checked on the china pot of steeping tea. Looked done, just the way Mother liked it.

She loaded the tea tray, her mind drifting. She'd lived on this ranch for so long, she hardly thought of the past anymore, or wondered what her life would have been like had she made different choices, if she hadn't let her mother talk her into doing the dutiful thing. Aumaleigh frowned, put a few crackers from the tin on a plate. She stared out the window. It did no good to look back and second guess the past, but she had regrets.

Big regrets.

As she reached for the sugar bowl, she saw the ranch foreman clomp into sight. Big and brawny, handsome in a can-do cowboy kind of way, Beckett Kincaid tromped up the steps, his dark hair scattering in the wind, his square jaw tensed. Looked like something was wrong.

Her stomach twisted. She knew exactly what it was. She quickly added a silver spoon to Mother's tray and turned just as the back door swung open, and Beckett filled the doorway. In his early thirties, Beckett was as handsome as they came. Men his age often made her wonder, if she'd made other choices, if she would have had a son. And if she did, then likely he would have been the same age as Beckett. A son with deep gray eyes, just like his pa—

Not that she ever let herself think of such things, of course. Her chin went up, she buried all thoughts of sons and marriages and lost opportunities and swept the tray off the counter. "Beckett. I recognize that look. I know why you're here."

"It's after noon on the first of the month, and I have a lot of unhappy cowboys asking me about their wages. Again. This is becoming commonplace." Beckett shut the door and managed to look apologetic and determined at the same time. Beckett was a good man. Understanding glinted in his gaze as he strolled forward, into the reach of the lamplight. He cleared his throat. "I have to ask if the pay is ready."

"No. Mother has been sleeping on and off all day." Aumaleigh set the tray on the nearby worktable, staring down at the fine china and silver, at the imported linens Mother had insisted on having. Only the very best for her. Aumaleigh sighed, ashamed of her mother's attitude toward others. "I've already checked with the bank. Mother is the only name on the account. Even if she is infirm, they will not let me sign for her."

"You mean, she won't give you permission to." Hard those words, said between clenched teeth, but that same understanding remained in his gaze. And maybe a dash of something else. Pity.

Yes, she knew how others saw her. The poor, spinster daughter, silently enduring her mother's sharp tongue and frequent wrath. How many times had she vowed not to put up with it anymore? How many times had she packed her bags or stood on the front steps of the little town bank ready to withdraw every penny of her savings and start a new life? But something always stopped her, or if it didn't, something inside her held her back. In the end, Maureen had no one else who would take care of her, and this was a daughter's duty.

With a sigh, she thought of the bank ledgers upstairs. Thought of the money her mother squirreled away with greedy self-interest, hating every penny she had to spend on others, even the wages they'd earned.

"I feel for you and the men, I really do," she said as gently as she could. "I'd hand out their pay this very instant if I could."

"She's simply not going to pay us then?"

"No. I'll talk to her about it again after her tea. Maybe she'll agree to it if I take the account book to her and put a pen in her hand." She shrugged. "I don't know what else I can do. When Maebry comes back from the May Day party, I plan to head to town. Nate may be able to help."

"I appreciate that, Aumaleigh. Thanks. An attorney was our next step." Beckett looked relieved, but still troubled. He owed it to his men to make sure they were fairly paid. "I don't know how many of them will stay, if I can't hand over their wages."

"I understand. Please give them my apologies. If there's nothing Nate can do, then I'll dig into my savings and pay everyone who is owed. Please tell them that."

"You shouldn't have to do that." Beckett's jaw clenched harder. "But thank you, Aumaleigh. Some of the men have families and they are hurting."

"I know." She felt bad for that. How did she explain all the times she'd said as much to her mother? Then again, Beckett nodded as if he already knew. He donned his hat, tipped it to her, and strode out of the kitchen. The door clicked behind him, leaving her alone.

A faint jangle from a hand bell penetrated the ceiling boards.

"Aumaleigh!" Mother shouted. "Where did you get off to! Where's my tea?"

"Coming." She scooped up the tray and hurried upstairs, dread growing with every step. She loved her mother, she always would, but she certainly didn't like the woman very much. A hard thing, a complicated thing. When she breezed into the over-warm bedroom where the fire crackled and popped, she did her best to shield her heart. Ignore the barbs, try to do the right thing.

"There you are." The corner of Mother's mouth hung low in one corner, more obvious than before. She wheezed, struggling to breathe. "I am tired of looking at you, and I need my tea. Where's Maebry? Why isn't she here to serve me?"

"She's helping with Nora's party, remember?" Calmly, Aumaleigh slid the tray onto the nightstand, shook out the lace-edged napkin and spread it out beneath her mother's chin. "She should be back soon."

"I heard the door open, I thought it was her." Mother managed a half-faced scowl. "She should be here. I need her. Who does she think she is?"

"Here, Mother." Aumaleigh ignored the tirade, measured out sugar cubes from the bowl and stirred them into the fragrant tea. "This will taste good. Are you hungry? I can get you a sandwich if you'd like. You hardly touched your lunch."

"That's because you were here. I want Maebry." Mother clamped her mouth together, raising her weakened hand to shove roughly at the tea cup. Nearly spilling it on herself.

Aumaleigh whisked it away just in time, ignoring the scalding liquid sloshing onto her hand. She calmly set saucer and cup down and reached for a second napkin, wiping the hot tea from her skin.

"I suppose I know who came. One of the men." Mother's face turned pink, her voice wobbling with anger. "Wanting his wages. Thinking only of himself. Selfish. That's all those people do, shirk on their work, do as little as possible, but when it comes time for their pay, they'd rob you blind if they could."

"You are two months behind paying them." Aumaleigh thought of the checkbook in the next room. She itched to get up and fetch it right now, but Mother had to calm down first. She could be stubborn.

A knock sounded on the back door, brisk and strong, ringing through the house. None of the ranch hands knocked, so who could it be? Most folks in town were at the Montgomery's party. Aumaleigh pushed off the bed. "I'll be right back."

"Did I say you could leave?" Mother arched one brow, lips pursed, commanding. "You'll sit right here and serve me. One of the maids will get the door."

Impossible, as she'd given then the afternoon off. Aumaleigh rolled her eyes. But what her mother didn't know, didn't hurt anyone. She pushed to her feet. "Is there anything else you want from downstairs?"

"A new daughter." Maureen smiled, as if sure her words had hit their mark.

Gone was the day such a thing would hurt. She crossed the room, feeling wooden and drained and hurried down the hallway. A man's shadowed figure stood at the bottom of the stairwell, looking up at her. That was a surprise.

"Aumaleigh." Nate Denby bobbed his head once in greeting, causing his glasses to slide down his nose a few inches. "I thought you might be busy, so I let myself in."

"Glad you did." As it had saved her a few steps. "Come on up. You must need to speak with my mother?"

"Yes. She wanted a few last minute things done to her will. A codicil." Nate patted a packet of papers he carried, taking the steps easily. "Is she awake?"

"Yes. I'll come down. There's something I want to talk to you about."

"The will?" Nate lowered his voice, backed away to allow her to pass. "You look exhausted. You must have been up all night with her."

"Maebry was already so worn out, I couldn't let her spell me." Aumaleigh ached, thinking of the young woman. She lowered her voice so it wouldn't carry up to mother. "Is there any way we can free Maebry now? When I inherit, I'll forgive the debt and have you dissolve the contract—"

"Oh, you don't know." Nate's face fell. "I'm sorry. I just assumed you'd overheard, since Maureen assured me she'd discussed this with you. Apparently she was less than honest."

"Not unusual for Mother."

"No." Nate dipped his chin, wincing, as if he wasn't happy to be the bearer of bad news. "Your mother changed her will. You should know that you are no longer named as her heir. She said you weren't deserving, that was her reason to me. So you will inherit nothing."

"Nothing?" She swallowed, jaw dropping, knees shaking. "Not even Maebry's contract?"

"No." Sympathy crinkled around his eyes. He reached out, caught her elbow, as if he knew she was about ready to fall. "Let me guess. That was the only thing you wanted from your mother, Maebry's contract."

"Yes. I asked her for it specifically. Just that." Tears filled her eyes, but not for herself. Oh, she didn't care about any inheritance. She didn't covet this place, she didn't give a hoot about all the money Mother squirreled away so selfishly. Not at all, not one cent.

It was Maebry she cared about and the hired people on this ranch who deserved to be paid the wages they'd worked for. Distraught for them, she blinked away her tears. "This is so unfair. Maebry deserves all the love Gil can give her."

"My sentiments exactly." Nate leaned in, studying her, the sweet young man that he was. "Are you all right?"

"Yes. Fine." She waved him away, now that the shock was over she was better. Stronger. "I'll leave you two alone to talk. Maybe you can ask her for me, one last time. I just want Maebry's contract, or for her to set her free in the will."

"I can try. I'll do my best." Nate drew in a deep breath as if gathering his courage to meet with the difficult woman and headed up the stairs.

Still shocked at her mother's cruelty, Aumaleigh crossed the kitchen, needing to start supper for the hired hands. Not that her mother's cruelty surprised her, but even after death? Maebry had done the work of two women, never complained, and this is the way Maureen treated her? It would have cost her nothing to dissolve the contract at her death, and yet she'd refused to do so. Oh, that made her so mad. Aumaleigh clenched her jaw, slapped a kettle on the stovetop, drowning in disappointment for Maebry, but Maureen loved money. Perhaps that would be an incentive for her to say yes, to let Gil buy Maebry's freedom.

Hoping so with all of her heart, Aumaleigh reached for a kettle. Above the clunk and clatter as she set it on the stove, Maureen's voice cut through the ceiling, blade-sharp.

"No! I said no." Anger rang in that thin voice, ugly and all consuming. "Without me, she'd be nothing but Irish trash living in squalor. This is all about some man, isn't it? That's a big mistake. Men always are. No, she'll thank me later for saving her from that. Mark my words, she'll thank me."

Oh yes, I've heard this before. Aumaleigh bowed her head, struggling not to remember when those words had been spoken about her and the man she once loved. It still hurt after all these years.

CHAPTER EIGHT

Maebry didn't know how long she spent in Gil's arms, cradled against him with the faint background of the party going on inside the house. All she knew was the precious warmth of him, the solid masculine feel, the scent of hay on his coat, the cadence of his every breath. His heartbeat became hers. For this one moment, he was her whole world. She felt so close to him, she didn't know where she stopped and he started.

Finally, a nearby door squeaked open. They were no longer alone. She felt Gil tense, felt him grimace as if he was as loath to let go as she was.

"Gil?" A man's voice said quietly. "I hate to interrupt, but I've been looking for you."

"You need help with the horses?" Regret rang in his voice, in his baritone that seemed to rumble through him.

Maebry stepped out of his arms, embarrassed at being caught so intimately, so privately, but the connection between them remained. He breathed, she breathed. His heart beat, hers did too. Some things could not be diminished by distance. She wrapped her arms around her waist, not sure what to do about this deepening affection she had for him. She had no right wanting him forever, not when she loved him so much.

"No." Tiernan shook his head, his gaze perceptive, nodding as if this was what he'd suspected all along, Gil's affection for her. The younger man straightened his tie, looking like the wealthy Montgomery's youngest son he was in his finely tailored clothing. "Some folks are leaving early, due to the bad roads, wanting to get home in the heat of the day. So we won't have a sudden rush of everyone leaving at once, horses and sleighs to juggle. So why don't you leave now? I can handle it."

"Only if you're sure." Gil stood tall, feet planted, hands on hips, powerful. The slight breeze tousled his dark hair, and even in his Sunday best he looked out of place on the genteel back porch full of wicker furniture and floral cushions and potted flowers blooming through the cold. There was something elemental about him, intensely male, as if not even the wide open plains could hold him.

If only he could be hers. That wish rose up, unbidden, straight from her soul. She bit her bottom lip, struggling to fight that dream. Best to be practical, to do the right thing for him. She took a step back, let the cool winds batter her body, tried to turn off the quiet dreams she didn't dare give into.

While Gil and Tiernan talked, she spun away, pressed against the damp, wooden banister, watched snowmelt drip from the roofline and onto the covered rose bushes below. The gardener had obviously taken care to protect the plants once it had started snowing.

She shivered, the ruffle of her white apron dancing in the breeze, remembering the winds back home ruffling her skirts while her parents fought. She lifted her face to the warm sunshine, felt its heat. Even as it shone brightly, it could not quite chase away all the remaining chill. Like a sign. That regardless of how her love shone, it wouldn't be enough. She'd seen it before.

"Maebry?" Gil's hand on her shoulder, the comfort of his touch. His big body leaned in, pressing against her with comfort, as if he knew she needed it. "C'mon, let's go. I'll take you home."

"Okay." Home. That was a good idea. She pushed away from the rail and from him in a daze, realizing she still wore the borrowed maid's uniform. "I have to change."

"Okay. I'll get Casey and wait for you out front." Gil's steady blue eyes held a note of sorrow. She felt his gaze on her back as she scurried away from him, running away.

Memories from her childhood threatened to surface as she grasped the door handle, yanked the door open and leaped inside. Once Gil was out of her sight, these strident, overwhelming emotions would ease up, right? She hurried down the hallway and into the small changing room, but the connection she felt to him, the bond between his heart and hers, did not lessen. She felt him as if he were standing with her, as if she were wrapped safely and snugly in his arms once again.

Longing filled her. She untied her apron and hung it on a nearby wall peg, thinking of the man waiting for her. What was she going to do? She unbuttoned the black frock, hung it up, reached for her old worn dress. She wanted to be in Gil's arms so much, missing him was a physical pain.

As she poked her arms through her dress sleeves, the door to the small room opened.

"I came looking for you and noticed you and Gil on the back porch. Together." Sarah Combs waggled her brows, her brown-red hair tumbling down in artful wispy corkscrew curls from a fancy up knot. "Very close together."

"You saw that?" Who else had, she wondered? Or had Tiernan said something.

"Oh, don't worry. The party is on the other side of the house." Sarah's eyes sparkled with friendliness behind her round spectacles. "Good thing, since you know this town. The Bluebell gossip mill is a thing to behold. Faster than greased lightning. I just wanted to give you my congratulations. Gil is a fine man, and he looks terribly serious about you."

"Yes, he is." On both counts. She buttoned up, a little embarrassed, a little chagrined.

"Hmm, does that mean you're not? Because from the look of things, you seemed pretty serious, too." Sarah removed Maebry's old coat from its peg. "Or am I wrong?"

"Oh, you're not wrong." Maebry gratefully took her coat and shrugged into it. "I don't think I'm the right one for Gil, for his future."

"Oh. The contract. Right." Sarah nodded, realization crossing her apple-cheeked face. "Well, he looks like a man determined to do whatever it takes for you. A woman couldn't ask for more."

"I know." Men didn't get better than Gil. As for the strength of his love—she squeezed her eyes tight for just a moment, to keep the wash of emotion in. "How are you doing? You must be glad the school year is almost over?"

"Can't wait, although my little natives are getting restless." She laughed, a warm, musical lilting sound. Infectious. "Something tells me Gil is waiting for you. Is he taking you home?"

"That's what he said." She wasn't sure how a wagon or a sleigh could get through the mire the roads would likely be in this thaw, so she shrugged. "At least you can walk home if you have to."

"Hey, I walked here. I had offers from a few gentleman to drive me, but honestly, I'm not sure about the choices in this town. At least I keep garnering the attention of the old, weak and infirm. Even though I'm happy being a spinster, it's hard on my ego."

"Oh, I don't know." She followed Sarah out the door and into the hallway. "Besides, there's always Lawrence Latimer."

"Oh, don't even mention that man." Sarah rolled her eyes, shaking her head. "He's proposed to me twice now. What can I say, he's just not my type."

"But he is persistent, I have to give him that." Maebry could have talked for hours, she didn't want to say goodbye. "Gil is waiting for me. I'd better go."

"Okay. But whatever is making you look so sad, it will all work out. I'm sure of it." She waltzed away in her pretty blue dress, waggling her brows.

What Sarah needed was a man as wonderful as Gil, Maebry thought as she trudged in the opposite direction, letting herself out onto the back porch. She truly wished that for her. Blinking through the bright sunshine, she made her way around the house. The first sight of Gil astride his gelding, sitting straight and commanding in the saddle made her eyes burn.

She wanted him. She wanted a future with him.

She wanted it too much.

"Hey, there." Gil reached down, his gloved hand engulfing hers. He slipped his foot out of his stirrup for her to use. His touch should quiet the turmoil she felt inside, but it did not. "With these roads, I thought it would be better to ride."

"Yes," she agreed. She read something new in his self-possessed, unwavering gaze. His love, like the bond between them, had grown. She could not miss his gaze as she hiked her foot into the stirrup and he lifted her up effortlessly, settling her in front of him, sidesaddle. His rock-hewn arms encircled her, holding her tight and safe, keeping her from falling. It felt wonderful. Blissful.

Any way she chose to break this off would hurt him immeasurably. She cringed inside, wishing she'd been smart enough not to let this happen in the first place, hating herself for not holding onto her resolve. As Casey started out in a regal walk, splashing down the muddy drive and onto the residential road, she wanted to call herself all sorts of names. The last thing she ever wanted was to hurt her beloved Gil.

So she buried her face against his shoulder, into the crook of his neck, and breathed him in. The male scent of his skin, the faint smell of soap in his clothes, the sensation of being close to him. This moment in time was the last she could have with him. She'd already decided that. Now it was only the matter of how she would break things off with him. Because she loved him.

***

He could sense the change in her as he reined Casey down the street. Kids played in yards, throwing the last snowballs of the year or rolling the last snowmen. Their calls and shouts filled the silence that had settled between him and Maebry.

She felt amazing in his arms, like hugging a little piece of heaven. So sweet and special, he lacked the words to express exactly how committed he was to her. But he couldn't forget her distress. His nerve endings felt on edge, his pulse drumming too quick, worrying over what was to come. He gritted his teeth until his jaw hurt. If she wouldn't let him go into debt for her, then how could they ever be together?

His chest cracked apart at the thought of living his life without her. Agony racked through him in blade-sharp stabs. He tightened his grip on her, holding her as close as he could. Time passed while Casey marched through mud and snowmelt and the sun slid behind a bank of clouds. One thing was clear. His world would end without her. It would come crashing down, shattering into pieces, never to be the same again.

He'd come too far to lose her, he thought resolutely. As the buildings of town ambled by, he tried to keep the bad possibilities out, focusing on this moment, on the sweet scent of lilacs in her silken hair, of the sensation of those golden strands catching on his whiskered jaw, on the sweetness of her soft, feminine form in his arms. He had to make this moment last; he needed to turn it into forever. As soon as town was behind them, he pressed a kiss into Maebry's hair, closed his eyes, wished he could tell her how much she meant to him. Hoped she wasn't planning on pushing him away.

"Gil?" A man's voice carried on the wind, a familiar one.

He blinked, looked up, spotted a bay horse heading in his direction down the muddy, tree-lined road. Easy to recognize the spectacled man riding closer, dark hair tousled by the wind. Nathaniel Denby looked grim as he held up one hand in greeting.

Uh oh. That didn't look good. Gil's stomach dropped. He felt his world begin to shatter, one breath at a time. "Nate. Looks like you are coming from the Rocking M."

"That's right." Nate stopped his horse so they were facing each other. Sadness marked his square face. He swept off his hat, respectfully, and something in his posture made Gil stop, made him set aside his troubles and see there was something else going on. Nate hung his head, cleared his throat. "I'm afraid I have bad news."

Gil turned cold inside. "It's Maureen?"

Nate nodded. He raised his head, took a breath. "She passed away a little bit ago."

"Oh, no." Maebry's hands flew to her face, she sat as still as stone, struck by the news. So tender-hearted. Gil curled his hand around her shoulder, felt her tremble, gave her a comforting squeeze.

"I'm sorry." Nate looked choked up. "I stayed with Aumaleigh as long as she would let me. Josslyn came in to help with supper, and she took over. She could do more for Aumaleigh, as they are so close. I feel as if there is more I should do. If you think of anything, will you tell me?"

"I will." Gil nodded once in thanks. "This will be hard on Aumaleigh."

"Yes, that's true." Nate's horse stepped forward a few paces, then stopped. The lawyer glanced over his shoulder, genuinely distressed. "I wish there was more I could do for you, Maebry. Maureen refused to consider giving you your freedom in her will. Aumaleigh isn't in a position to negotiate on the estate's behalf."

"I know." Maebry nodded matter-of-factly, as if this was no surprise to her at all. "Thanks anyway, Nate, for trying. That was decent of you."

"It's not right how this turned out." Troubled, Nate urged his horse on, riding through the shadows, heading toward town.

Sorrow for Maureen and especially for Aumaleigh battered him.

Gil blinked once, trying to keep it all in, but it was nothing compared to the wrench of loss he felt for Maebry. What was to become of her? The bottom fell out of his stomach. He felt as if he were falling, tumbling, unable to stop. He let out a shaky breath.

"I need to get home, Gil." Maebry sounded different, her voice without music, without emotion. She stared ahead toward the bend in the road, where the hills arched upward toward the sky, hiding the ranch's main buildings from sight. "I need to help Aumaleigh. She shouldn't have to deal with this all alone. The death, preparing the body. The wake and the f-funeral."

Maebry was crying. Controlled, honest tears she fought to hold back. But they came anyway, escaping over her bottom lashes to roll slowly down her cheeks.

Crying for Maureen. Crying for Aumaleigh.

And for us, he thought. She would never accept the love and future he wanted to offer her. Holding his heart still, so still he couldn't feel a thing, he urged Casey forward, racing home.

CHAPTER NINE

Aumaleigh sat in the silent room alone with her mother's body. The bright red rage that had dominated Maureen's face less than thirty minutes ago had faded, her tirade over refusing to accept Nate's suggestion to give Maebry her freedom had long since silenced, only the evidence of her final stroke remained in the unnatural twist of her face.

Aumaleigh let out a sad sigh that was part sob. She felt sorry for her mother, she felt deep pity for her mother, she wished things had gone differently for her. But it would be hard to miss her. No, she thought as she brushed an errant white curl off her mother's forehead, she'd been grieving for years. Grieving for the mother Maureen failed to be, grieving for the happiness Mother could have had if she'd softened her heart, grieving for the love, every bit of it, Maureen had shoved away and dismissed as worthless.

All the money Maureen had saved up, stowing away with a miser's love, did her no good now. That was the true tragedy of Maureen McPhee's life. Aumaleigh patted the cold, gnarled hand, sad that her mother had run out of chances to redeem her life, to finally understand what mattered.

Exhausted, Aumaleigh stood, the only sounds in the room were the faint squeak of the bed ropes, the slow cadence of her shoes across the floorboards, the pop from the fireplace where the fire had burned down to embers and ashes. Even with her mother gone, she still knelt to add wood to the grate, reached for the steel poker to stir up the embers, feeling the radiant heat against her face. She did not want to leave the body in a cold room.

She blinked back tears, it was time to say goodbye. She studied the empty shell, pathetic looking now with Mother's malice gone. The room seemed almost peaceful. Perhaps wherever Maureen's soul was now, she'd found some semblance of peace. Hoping so, Aumaleigh swiped hot tears from her eyes, reached out and patted her mother's foot through the bed covers.

"It wasn't easy loving you, but I did." The words stuck like paste in her throat. But she said them anyway. "Have a good journey."

She wished things could have been different, but they could not be changed now. She had to accept that. She'd done all she could for Mother. Everything a daughter could do. And it was over now. Feeling a little hollow, a little grateful and mostly relieved, she retreated from the bed and headed for the door.

Josslyn and Orla were in the hall, carrying towels, clothes and a basin of steaming water. Both sorrow and understanding wreathed their faces.

"We'll take care of her." Josslyn reached out, patted Aumaleigh's arm, her touch communicating decades of friendship. "You go downstairs and let this soak in. I left some tea on the table for you. Drink it, and I'll be down to talk in a bit."

Tears flooded Aumaleigh's eyes. She didn't know what to say. "What would I ever do without you?"

"You'll never have to find out." Josslyn scooted by her in the narrow hall.

"That's right," Orla seconded. Water sloshed out of the basin as she switched hands, reached out to give Aumaleigh a brief, comforting hug. "We're right here, right beside you. We aren't going anywhere."

"Even when it looks like you won't get paid now?" she joked, choosing humor over tears, but they came anyway. She gave Orla another hug, exchanged looks with Josslyn that she hoped communicated her love and gratitude and stumbled down the hall, spared the sad task of washing and preparing her mother's body.

The stairs ahead of her blurred, growing more impossible to see with every step. She grasped the railing tightly as she went down the stairs and willed the tears from her eyes, but the searing wetness brimmed over, unstoppable. She felt her way across the kitchen to the little drop-leaf table by the side window. She groped her way into one of the chairs, breathed in the scented steam of the steeping tea—the lavender and chamomile blend she made from her own garden—and planted her elbows on the table. Lowering her face into her hands, she let the tears come. She cried for Maureen's wasted life; she cried for herself and for the love that she'd lost, the love that would never come around again.

* * *

When the two story log house came into sight with lamplight gleaming in the windows and gray smoke curling up from chimneys and stove pipes, Maebry felt the unrelenting hit of surprising sorrow. Mourning seemed to hover around the house, darkening the light, feeding the shadows.

Feeling full of shadows herself, her heart caught on a beat, lingering there, stuttering. It was her future that troubled her now and she hung her head as Casey eased to a slow walk. His rolling gate rocked her against Gil's broad chest one last time before the animal stopped on the drive between the house and the nearest barn. She clung to the saddle horn, in her mind she'd already leaped from the horse's back and stood on the ground...except she hadn't moved a muscle.

Probably because she didn't want to. Sorrow ratcheted through her. She knew that her life would be worse with Maureen gone. Things had to be different now. Maebry blew out a breath, forced herself to unwrap her fingers from around the leather horn. Time to get out of this saddle and away from Gil. Like Cinderella, her clock had struck midnight. It was back to the reality of her life, to the consequences she'd chosen long ago when she'd signed seven years of her life over to Maureen, and seven more for Nia.

She hiked her chin up, noticed Gil had slipped his foot from one of his stirrups for her to use. Remnants of their time together, of that long, endless, timeless span on the porch in his arms, simply being held by him, stayed with her. And hurt as she stuck her toes into the stirrup, took care not to lean on Gil, not to need him as she climbed down.

He sensed it. She knew he did. It was like the sun going out. Like the world had stopped spinning.

"Thank you for the ride home." Polite, courteous, distant. That's how it had to be. She fisted her hands for strength, took a step in the mud, felt it squish beneath the soles of her shoes. "Thanks to you too, Casey. You braved all that mud fearlessly."

Casey arched his neck, gave a little proud nicker as if to say in his horsy way, *no problem*.

"You'll let me know if you need anything?" Gil's kindness reached out to her, stopping her in her tracks.

Oh, she wanted him. She squeezed her eyes shut, willing every muscle in her body *not* to turn around, not give in to the temptation to gaze upon him. Already she missed him, the heat of his presence, the snap of connection zinging through her heart. She *needed* to look into his eyes and read his feelings there. He was her weakness, this love she felt was hopeless. She belonged to strangers, now, to people who lived in Illinois, who controlled her destiny. She knew nothing about Maureen's heirs. Not one thing.

She did her best to keep walking, to nod, raise her hand in acknowledgement, but she kept on going. Squishing through the mud, fighting her feelings, doing what she had to do. The right thing to do. The only thing she could do.

As if Gil understood, he didn't call out to her again. The world felt cold, the wind hostile as she plunged one foot into the thick mire, heard the splash of water, wished her heart wasn't shattering into a million pieces. Didn't know how to stop it. She longed for the safe harbor of Gil's arms with every fiber of her being.

Be stronger, Maebry, she told herself as she took another step. The twine holding her shoe snapped, the leather encasing her foot loosened, and the cold ooze seeped in. She gave a tug, but the shoe stayed stuck in the mud, her stockinged foot slid out, coated with mud. Oh, no, not again. She stood in place, balancing on one foot. He was watching her, she could feel Gil's gaze, the weight of it, the caress of it. So she did the only thing she could. She grabbed her lost shoe and kept on walking. More mud oozed between her toes (yes, this stocking had a hole in it too, she was still behind on her darning) but she ignored it. Perhaps Gil would do the right thing too and keep on riding toward the barn.

"What are you doing?" he called out. His caring, his kindness felt cruel. Like the taunt of a hot summer's day, the teasing flutter of a summery breeze in mid-winter. She heard the saddle leather creak as he dismounted, heard the splash and patter of his boots in the mud behind her, barricaded her heart so his wonderful tenderness wouldn't affect her, so she could keep all the love she felt for him walled in.

It did no good. The heat of his hand when it landed on her shoulder burned through layers of wool and flannel to the skin beneath, telegraphing his rare, dependable sort of comfort—the exact thing she hungered for. The one thing she could not let herself have. Struggling to hold onto her dignity, she hopped up the steps and onto the porch, leaving muddy prints in her wake.

"Maebry." He caught up to her, grabbed her elbow, spun her around. It hurt to see the concern dug in around his eyes, to hear the thick rumble of affection when he said her name. "You should have waited for me. I would have carried you."

"I know." Wasn't that what tortured her the most? That she'd found the right man, the one she would love through her lifetime, but she had nine years left to serve on her contract, nine years worth of debt to pay off. To strangers now, people who could move her to Chicago. She had no say in that. She'd signed a legal agreement, and now they had inherited that agreement. She didn't need to ask Nate to know that for a fact. She drew in a shaky breath, staring hard at one of Gil's coat buttons so she wouldn't have to meet his gaze. "I prefer to walk on my own."

"Through the mud?"

"Through the mud. It's not so bad. I'm sure it's good for my skin and calluses." A feeble attempt at humor. It fell short, and she shrugged. "It's better this way, Gil."

"Sorry, I don't buy that." He rubbed his knuckles against her jaw, moving closer, shadowing her with his height and strength. "I know Nate will contact the heirs, and he'll give them my offer too. He knows how serious I am."

"That's the thing." She reached out, splayed her hand on his hard chest, keeping him from moving in closer. It took a Herculean effort to meet his gaze, to see the tenacious hope there, the true devotion, the pain of her rejection. Oh, she did not want to hurt him. That's why she had to do what was right. "You have to let this go."

"Not as long as I can see love in your eyes, love for me." His hand covered hers, holding her palm against the steady thud of his heartbeat. He drew himself up to full height, like a man who refused to stop fighting to love her. "I won't let you go, Maebry."

His fingers covering hers squeezed meaningfully. In his eyes shone his dreams for their future. For love, marriage and family. The hope for a happily-ever-after.

Oh, she wanted those dreams too. Little girls with Gil's true blue eyes, little boys with dark hair and his goodness. Laughter and togetherness and year after year spent loving this man, this loyal, strong man. She blew out a shaky breath, took a few moments to feel the life-affirming rhythm of his heartbeat. Funny how hers beat in time with his. As if they were one.

Always would be.

"What choice do we have? I watched my parents struggle with terrible debt." The confession came thin and raw, full of emotion. Tough memories from her childhood, the one she worked to forget. He had to understand. "My mother's family struggled to hold onto their land. It wasn't much, but it was enough to make a living. There had been illness, and then gambling debts, all borrowed against the land. My father, oh, he was a dreamer. He said it didn't matter, he'd marry my mother, work to pay off the debt, that only love mattered."

"Let me guess." Gil's free hand cupped her jaw, cradling her, oh so tender. "It didn't work out that way."

"No. It was a hardship, a black mark against them from the start. They both worked their fingers to the bone. There was nothing but work and hardship and despair." She closed her mind against the arguments, the disappointments, the shell of disenchantment her parent's marriage became. "I watched it all. How my father gradually came to resent my mother. He'd sacrificed so much for her, after all. My mother resented him for not loving her enough, the way he'd promised. My father died a broken man, and my mother turned bitter, lost her heart."

"And you think that will be us?" Gentle, those words, wanting to understand. "You're afraid that I will come to resent you, that instead of you I could have had my own ranch? Or maybe a wife who wasn't such a burden?"

"Yes." *Finally*. Relief rocked through her like lightning striking, threatened to knock her to her knees. Tears flooded her eyes. Now that he understood, he could stop trying to rescue her. She never wanted to be something he regretted. "It was nice while it lasted. You have no idea what you mean to me. I'm really glad I let down my guards and let you in."

"Me, too." Tears stood in his eyes, a rare show of the deepest layer of his heart, tears he blinked away, stalwart. Invincible.

Heart shattering, she went up on tiptoe, kissed his cheek, ignored the catch of longing in her chest. With her shoe clutched in her other hand, she turned on her heel, leaving him alone on the porch. As she stepped into the kitchen and closed the door behind her, the sun chose that moment to disappear fully behind encroaching clouds, leaving the day as if in twilight. Like a sign.

Their chance at love had passed.

* * *

Gil closed Casey's stall gate, double-checking to make sure it had locked. At least now he understood why Maebry had been so upset over his offer to buy out her contract. Heartbroken, at a loss, he scrubbed the gelding's nose a final time, grabbed the empty grain bucket and headed down the aisle. Casey's nicker of good-night followed him, along with the questioning and neighs of a barn full of horses who heard the rattle of the pail's handle and poked their heads into the aisle, hoping for a bit more grain.

"Sorry, guys." He shrugged, showed them the empty bottom of the bucket, earned a few horsy huffs and raspberries. Seemed like everyone was in for disappointment tonight. He tossed the bucket into the feed room, blew out the last lantern and dug into his leather saddlebags on his way out the door for the package he'd picked up in town.

"Better hurry up!" Beckett Kincaid, ranch foreman extraordinaire, called out from the yard as he hiked up the hill, toward the small cottage he shared with his small daughter. "Everyone's already in there. There won't likely be any grub left by the time you get there."

"I'm not worried. I have an in with the cook." A cook who still owed him baked goods. A cool rain needled down from a swollen, charcoal sky as he wrestled the barn door shut.

"We'll be rounding up the horses soon, bringing in the prime ones to break." Beckett turned around, angling his hat to shield his face from the rain. "I'll need help. Are you interested?"

"Yes." His gaze cut to the kitchen window, shining in the encroaching darkness. Maebry was in there, the love of his life. If she thought he was going to let her go, then she was plain crazy. He splashed through the mud, changed the angle of his hat to catch the rain, winked at

Beckett. "I could use the extra work. You think we'll ever get paid for it?"

"I'll talk it over with Nate, Maureen's heirs will inherit her debts too. Haven't heard all the details of the will yet, the formal reading will be after the funeral, but it only stands to reason they'll either want to sell out their share of this place or make it work, and either way you have to pay ranch hands to run this place."

"Right." Gil shifted the package he carried to his other hand, stared down the shadowed valley, felt his future shift. "I may be giving my notice. Depends on where Maebry ends up."

"Okay. I understand. I was in love once." Becket backed up the path, into the dark. "We'll talk."

"Right." Gil felt the rain sluice against the side of his face like a touch. Funny how things worked out. Like his love for Maebry really was meant to be. He hiked across the yard, heading straight for that light, for Maebry, his life.

"There you are!" Orla whipped open the back door, pinned her gaze on him and shook her head in mock disapproval. "Supper is on the table."

"I just want a plate, if that's okay with you." He hiked up the steps, stomped the mud off his boots. "I'll eat in the bunkhouse."

"That's understandable, considering." Orla nodded, wearing an apron, holding a wooden spoon. She stepped back from the doorway to make way for him. "What with Maureen's passing and the news about Maebry. Poor Maebry. What if they want to take her from us? I don't think I can let that girl go. She's like a daughter to me. Now you just come in where it's warm, stand right there, don't touch that cake. I'll dish you up a plate."

"Thanks, Orla." He swept off his hat, shouldered the door shut and breathed in the delicious aromas of chicken, dumplings and lemon cake. His stomach grumbled, but food wasn't foremost on his mind. He searched the room for signs of Maebry, strained to hear the lilt of her voice in the nearby dining room. A faint pad of footsteps in the room overhead grabbed his attention. There she was, upstairs probably helping Aumaleigh.

"I'll just be a minute," Orla called over her shoulder as she bustled across the room, a clean plate in hand. "All the food is on the table. I'll load up and be right back."

"Great." He waited until she was out of sight before grasping the glass knob on the door to his left. Maebry's room. It was dark and cool, her narrow bed neatly made, the pillow plumped, a worn and patched wool blanket folded over the foot of the mattress. A tiny room, little more than a closet. His chest twisted as he crossed to the bed. She deserved better than this, and he would give it to her.

He unwrapped the brown paper, the gift he'd left the Montgomery's party to buy. He set the pair of shoes on the blanket at the foot of the bed, brand new. Her exact size. The best pair in Gunderson's Mercantile. He hoped she would understand the meaning behind his gift as he left the room, closing the door behind him.

CHAPTER TEN

"There. We have everything ready." Maebry fussed with the lace scarf she'd draped over the side of the open coffin, so it would hang just right.

The big, open front room had once been the parlor when Maureen's family first lived here, then the dining room for the ranch hands when McPhee Manor up on the hill had been completed. Now the dozens of chairs had been moved into a smaller, adjacent room and the table supported Maureen's coffin. Sadness hung in the air, the reverence of life lost. Fire crackled in the stone hearth, crystal lamps beamed golden light, but cold and shadows remained, as if nothing could touch them.

"Yep, we're all ready for tomorrow." Orla seized the broom by its handle and headed toward the hallway. "Do you think anyone will show up?"

"Hard to say," Josslyn answered, with a supporting arm around Aumaleigh's slender waist. "We'll be here. That's something."

"Mother wasn't the kind of person who had friends as much as she had allies." Aumaleigh's sorrow was palpable, carved into her face, heavy on her shoulders. "I don't think we should expect a large gathering."

"That's sad." Maebry hung her head. Maureen had been a hard taskmaster, but she looked humble in death. Shrunken, skeletal, tiny. *I owe her so much*, she thought, reminding herself stoically of what was only the truth.

How would her life have turned out had she stayed in Ireland? A burden to her family who didn't have enough to eat, living under the cloud of her stepfather's anger and drinking problems. No, at least she'd made a good life for herself here and, more importantly, was able to help her only sister to a better life as well.

She really did owe Maureen so much. She just wished it hadn't cost her Gil. Fresh misery rolled through her as she padded in her stocking feet to the nearby lamp. Her fingers trembled as she lifted a glass chimney and blew out the flame. She stood in the dark, listening to the others tap away toward the kitchen. She squared her shoulders. What she needed was a good night's sleep to prepare for tomorrow, and what may come from there.

"I just wish I knew more about the heirs." Orla's voice trailed down the short hallway to the kitchen, where a closet door banged shut. She must be putting away the broom.

"Oh, I remember Ely's daughters from back in the day." Josslyn gently steered Aumaleigh away from the dark coffin where her mother's body rested and toward the light of the kitchen. "They were just little girls then, but sweet as could be. Ely's little Rose was my Seth's age. Just wee ones, tottering around. I'll never forget how they played together."

"I remember." Aumaleigh's voice was coarse from hours of crying, but she cleared her throat, spoke warmly. With love. "My nieces. Of course, they wouldn't remember me. I only visited a few times before Mother had enough of that. You know how she was good at getting her way."

"Do I," Orla commented, bustling to rescue the rumbling tea kettle from the stove. "I wish I'd met this Ely, but I hired on after he'd moved away."

"After Mother drove him away," Aumaleigh corrected. It was easy to read her unhappiness. "Those little girls were wonderful. Sweet and as pretty as could be. Iris was the oldest one. Strawberry blond hair, eyes as blue as periwinkles. Daisy came next, molasses-brown hair straight like mine, and blue eyes like her pa's."

"You love them still, don't you?" Maebry knew how that was, to love someone from afar. It's how she'd loved her sister, who was too far away to visit. It was how she would have to love Gil from now on. She pulled out a chair at the work table while Josslyn steered Aumaleigh into it.

"Yes, I still do." Aumaleigh settled her skirts, her face brightening. "They are all grown now, but I can remember them like it was yesterday. Little Rose with her blond curls and baby Magnolia with her sunny, golden hair. I never got to meet the last child, Verbena. It's funny how family binds your heart and time doesn't matter, even twenty years later."

"Do you think they'll come out to visit?" Maebry couldn't help asking. "They may want to see the land they've inherited."

"If they do, it would be lovely to see them again, it would mean so much." Aumaleigh swiped at her eyes, Aumaleigh who was now alone, without any family. "Look at me, going on. Who knows what the future will bring? Likely those young ladies are very sophisticated and polished, used to the comforts of a fine city. What would they want with a ranch?"

But Aumaleigh had her hopes up, Maebry could tell. She patted Aumaleigh's shoulder, rushing to help Orla pour the tea. Getting Aumaleigh through these tough few days was first and foremost, but she couldn't help wondering about the five young women who'd inherited her contract. Would they be pleasant to work for? She truly hoped so. It was almost too much to dream of, and the thought of leaving here, of leaving Gil, was too much to bear.

The floorboard felt cool against her stocking feet as she joined Orla at the kitchen counter. Weariness hung on her like the night shadows.

"Here, this is just what Aumaleigh needs." Orla handed over a steaming cup of tea. "Chamomile for sleep, lavender to relax, a dollop of honey to make her sweeter."

"Impossible, she's already sweet enough as she is." Gently teasing, but meaning every word, Maebry delivered the cup, squeezed Aumaleigh's hand in silent sympathy and remembered her work wasn't done yet. She still had her muddy shoe to wash out and leave by the stove to dry, hopefully before morning. No way could she be seen at Maureen's wake in her stockings.

"Maebry, you look asleep on your feet." Josslyn sidled over, concern lining her tired face. Maureen's passing weighed on her too. "Go on to bed, honey. I'll clean up here before going home."

"You've had a late night too, you look exhausted," she protested.

"I'm just fine, don't you worry about me." Josslyn opened Maebry's bedroom door. "Now get in there, go. I'm your supervisor, so you'd best do what I say or I'll fire you."

"Now you're just teasing me." Maebry rolled her eyes. "I can't be fired."

"Well, it's the only threat I have." Josslyn steered her through the doorway firmly, not one to be taken lightly. "I'll see you in the morning. Sleep well, and don't worry. This is all going to work out for the best."

"Why do you say that?" So much was up in the air, and while a woman had died and it was no time to be thinking of herself, Maebry couldn't help worrying about the uncertainty of her future.

"Because I remember those girls. I knew their parents well. Ely's wife Laura and I were friends back in the day, as was Aumaleigh. We were a threesome, us girls, sewing together on a winter afternoon or sitting out on the porch on a summer's evening. I know good people when I see them, and the girls who have inherited this place and your contract, they are good people."

"You knew them when they were small children." She kept her voice low, so it wouldn't carry to Aumaleigh, who was at the table trying to sip her tea while Orla supervised, lovingly watching over her. Maebry swallowed, trying to dislodge the lump in her throat. "A lot can change. They grew up in a big city. They're still strangers."

"Yes, but I have a good feeling." Josslyn's eyes shone, sure of that knowledge.

Maebry blew out a sigh, part relief, but wishing. It really would be nice to work for kinder people than Maureen had been. That was solace enough, the reassurance she needed to step into the dark room, face the darkness of another night alone.

"Look, there's something on your bed." Josslyn's surprise came warmly, not like there was something alarming like a snake or a giant spider on her blankets.

Maebry squinted through the faint path of light falling through the open door, bringing the shadowed images into focus. A new pair of shoes. Just sitting there, with no note, no explanation. She ran her fingertip across the fine leather, felt the bump of each carefully sewn button and seam. They were beautiful, amazing. Just the nicest things. She gathered them up in her arms and hugged them. She could not believe what he'd done.

"That Gil." Josslyn smiled understandingly.

Yes, Gil. Emotion gathered behind her eyes, hot and hard and blinding. Tenderness rushed through her, a love so strong nothing could diminish. It burned like a light not even darkness could put out, like a summer's day that had no end. She felt Gil's love, although he was nowhere near, like a whisper in her heart.

"Go to him," Josslyn advised, handing Maebry her coat. "Go."

Yes, she had some things to say to him. And it wasn't going to be easy.

* * *

There she is. Gil's pulse skidded to an utter and complete stop as he gazed across the front room of the bunkhouse at the darkly gleaming window. Her silhouette shone behind the room's reflection, slim, feminine, beautiful. What a sight.

"Excuse me, gentleman." He closed his book, set it aside and pushed himself out of the chair.

"Oohwee," Shep hooted, looking up from his dime novel. He waggled his eyebrows. "Look who's got himself a lady."

"It was just a matter of time," Kellan commented, turning a page in the *Deer Springs Gazette*. "He's been mooning after her since he got here."

"Women. Nothing but trouble." John Brockman, the gruff old cowboy, shook his head, lifted an empty tin can to his lips and spit out a stream of tobacco juice. "That's why I stay away from 'em. You'd be smart to do the same."

"Yeah, well no one ever called me smart." Gil wove around cowboys, stepped over their crossed feet, marched straight for the door.

Maebry stood in the muted light from the window, clutching the shoes he'd bought her to her chest. Oh, she about broke his heart standing there like a waif in the ragged clothing Maureen provided for her.

"Why aren't those on your feet?" he asked gently, already knowing her answer, already prepared for the rejection she'd surely come to give him. Well, he'd had enough of that, he thought tenderly, closing the door shut good and tight and moving in to her. He stared at her feet. "What are you wearing?"

"A pair of barn boots Shep left with Aumaleigh to mend." She shrugged, her carved, dainty chin hiking up a notch. Boy, was that girl stubborn. It only made him love her more. She pinched her forehead, furrows digging in as she raised apologetic green eyes to meet his. "I can't accept these, Gil. You know that."

"Well, I'm not going to take them back. You know that too." He brushed a stray blond curl from her face, tucking it behind the shell of her ear. "They'd look all wrong on me. Think what they'd do for my reputation. I'd never live it down."

"Don't even try to make me laugh." She made a small choking sound, almost like a sob, betraying her.

His dear, sweet Maebry. Affection lifted through him, powerful and everlasting. How he loved her. He smiled, felt the worry and fear of losing her fade from his chest. "That's how it always is with us, Sunshine. We make each other laugh. Don't think we should change that now."

"You mean, now that we have to go back to being friends?" A wobbly question, belying that strong, set angle of her jaw.

It had to be tough being an indentured servant for Maureen. Long, relentless workdays, a tough taskmaster, no kindness. But that was over now. He took hold of the shoes, the fine leather soft against his hand. He tugged, she let go, relieved.

Too bad she misunderstood.

"Thank you." She tilted her head back, gazing up at him, her shield slipping down. In that moment he saw everything, the quiet hopes she dared not wish for, what his gift meant to her, the love she tried to hide. Everlasting love for him. She blew out a shaky sigh, stepped back, as if trying to hide in the dark night. "I can't believe you're being so great about this. It really was very thoughtful of you, Gil."

"No, just showing you the way I intend to go." He caught her wrist before she could escape, wrapped his fingers around her arm, holding her firmly even when she tugged. She could fight, but some things in life could not be changed. His love for her was one of them.

"I'm going to take care of you," he told her, nudging her backward across the covered porch. "That's the way it's going to be."

"Oh, no, I'm suddenly getting flashes of Lawrence Latimer." She joked, trying to lighten the mood, trying to resist as he steered her through the darkness. "You two are more alike than I'd first thought."

"Honey, we are nothing alike." He towered over her, six feet plus of solid, invincible man. "Now sit down."

"And if I refuse?" She felt the edge of a chair's seat behind the back of her knees. Again, his kindness was killing her, tearing her apart. Making what she had to do much harder. "You can't be taking care of me, Gil."

"That's what you do when you love someone very, very much." He knelt down, set the new shoes on the shadowed porch boards and grabbed hold of the heel of the boot she wore. "Especially when you love someone so much, you'll never be able to stop."

"Oh, Gil." Her eyes smarted as she stared down at the man kneeling in front of her, head bowed, strong shoulders set, his hand on her heel. Weak, just too weak, she dropped into the chair. "What am I going to do with you?"

"You'll have to keep me, I guess." Cowboy humble, in his easygoing way, she felt his silent confession, the one that spoke in the silence behind his words, the deeper meaning that perhaps there were no words for. It was his heart touching hers. In the dark, he was more shadow, almost hidden to her.

His feelings were not. She covered her face with her hands, needing to hide her reaction from him. Didn't he understand what he was doing to her? Couldn't he see that if she would let herself dream, that he would be in every one of those dreams, at the very center, as the love of her life?

"If you don't keep me," he said, his baritone rumbling low and deep, "then who knows what will become of me? I might turn out as lovesick as Lawrence. Maybe become melancholy, lose my job, end up on the streets. Me and Casey walking through town begging for spare change."

"You're doing it again." She felt the boot slip off, the chilly night air on her foot, especially through the holes in her stocking (she really needed to find the time to fix all of her socks). "You're trying to make me laugh."

"Honey, that's my job, and I'm going to do it for the rest of your life." The boots hit the porch with a thud and the night deepened, as if to hide all signs of him. "You only have nine years left on your contract."

"Only nine years?" That made her laugh. She shook her head, only Gil could think nine years was a short time. "By then, I'll be twenty-nine, a month shy of thirty. You'll be thirty-four. You can't be serious."

"Deadly." He held her foot in his big hands, rested it on his solid knee. "I'll wait for you, Maebry. A lifetime if I have to."

"I can't ask you to. It's crazy. It's a long time, Gil. You might get tired of waiting."

"Now what did I just say?" Infinitely tender those words as he tugged on one new shoe, reached for her other foot. "A lifetime, Maebry. That's what you are to me. You are my life."

Amazing words. She drank in the sound of them, cherishing every ounce of his heart-felt feelings. She wanted to give in, she wanted to believe but all she saw was doom. Of him getting frustrated as time went by, of all the things in life he was missing out on by waiting for her—marriage, children, a happy family. The ranch he wanted to buy. All on hold, because of her. No, she shook her head, adamantly, fighting down a sob. She was not worth that.

"You are worth it." He slipped on her other shoe, lowered her foot to the ground, reached up to take her hand. How had he read her mind like that? How had he known? She opened her mouth to argue, to do what was best for him and convince him to let her go, when he cradled her hand in both of his. Something about the action stopped her short, made her pulse skip and realization zip through her like a lightning strike.

No, he couldn't be about to—"

"Maebry O'Riley, will you marry me?" He proposed, just like that, with all his love and devotion ringing in the rich, rumbling timbre of his deep voice. "You light up my life, without you there is only darkness. Please say yes."

"I wish I could," she whispered, unable to stop the tears spilling down her cheeks. "You have no idea."

Her future with him, that's what she couldn't let herself imagine, couldn't let even one wonderful image in. She fought against it, just as she fought the tears. She wanted him with everything in her soul, but how could she say yes? Worse, she thought, swiping at her eyes with her free hands, how could she say no? "I don't want to hurt you, Gil."

"Then don't. Because you will destroy me." Honest, without a drop of humor, utterly serious. He cradled her hand in his, raised it to his face, pressed a kiss to her knuckles. That kiss, more tender than any dream. "Why can't you say yes?"

"I don't know my future." Even as she resisted it, the doors on her heart eked open, the truth, so tender and vulnerable, needing to be said. "I care about you so much, Gil. More than myself, more than my life. I love you so very much. If I say no, then I hurt you. But if I say yes, I know I'll lose you. Nine years is a long time, and I don't think I could bear losing you. I just don't think I could."

She bowed her head, ashamed of her weakness for him, for a love so strong it had overthrown her heart, seized every piece of her soul.

"I see." Kind, those words. That was Gil, always kind, even when he had to be sensible, responsible, do the right thing. At least now he could see what the right thing was.

He brought her hand to his cheek, pressed it there for a moment, as if he finally understood there was no solution, no real way for their love to work out. Wrapped up in her own heartbreak, in the wrenching realization that she would never know the pleasure of being his fiancé, the thrill of being his wife, the happiness of raising a family with him, she didn't notice the ring he'd slipped onto her finger until the warm band of gold he'd taken from his pocket encircled her left fourth finger.

"This is the kind of love that lasts. Just let yourself believe." He leaned forward, brushed her cheek with the sweetest kiss. The truth lit his eyes, revealed his devotion to her, without end. "There is no way you're losing me, Sunshine. I'm sticking like mud to your shoe."

"Funny. I'm not fond of mud." She reached out, let her hand rest on the firm span of his shoulder, felt the change, the belief begin to fill her heart. This really was happening, his love for her was strong. As strong as her love for him.

Invincible.

"It's a metaphor," he told her, leaning in, the corners of his mouth crooking up into a dashing smile. "Maybe not the best one, but I'm a cowboy, not a poet."

"You're certainly no poet." She found herself leaning in too, needing him, dreaming of him. "Good thing too, as I'm fond of cowboys."

"Lucky me." He kissed the ring on her finger. His commitment to her the most tender thing she'd ever seen. "I'm going to love you forever."

"That's how I will love you, too." The ring on her finger was real, the dream of Gil Blackburn was hers. He wasn't going to let her go, he would wait for her. This was a solution she could live with. True love was sacrifice, and it was patience and it was forever. She read that all in his eyes, felt it in his heart. He would wait for her, and then they would be happy. So, so happy. She blinked through her tears. "Yes, Gil. I'll marry you."

"Good. Hope you know that I believe in long engagements," he teased, his lips hovering over hers. "Nine years sounds about right."

"That will give me plenty of time to plan our wedding," she joked right back, laughing when their lips met, when he kissed her with all the love in his heart.

That's how she kissed him too, with all the love in hers.

EPILOGUE

Three weeks later

"Hey, Maebry!" Sarah Combs called out from across the street as she sashayed merrily down the boardwalk in front of the feed store. "You look like a happily engaged woman."

"That's because I am," Maebry called back as she tied Phil's reins to the hitching post. She squinted through the sun, so bright and hot on this late May day. "You look thrilled school is out for the summer."

"Totally thrilled. I'm free!" Sarah held up a package. "Just bought the makings for a new hat. Got to keep busy."

"I want to see it when you're done." Maebry gave Phil a pat before hopping onto the boardwalk.

"I will!" Sarah promised and waved goodbye.

Feeling happy, truly happy, Maebry headed straight for Gunderson's Mercantile. The blazing heat, the chirp of birds, the better working conditions at the ranch were all a factor. Being engaged to Gil was another—and the biggest reason she was happier than she'd ever been.

The bell above the mercantile door chimed as she swished inside. Her new shoes tapped their way across the floorboards, light as air, as Gemma looked up from the counter.

"Why, you look positively radiant." Gemma flushed pink with happiness for her friend, bringing out her own quiet beauty. "Must be that pretty ring on your finger."

"Yes, the man who gave it to me has nothing to do with it," she joked.

"Yeah, I didn't think Gil had anything to do with that grin of yours." Gemma set down her pencil, closed her account book and circled around the front counter. She looked elegant and handsome in a rose colored dress. "Have you heard any word from Maureen's heirs?"

"No, but Nate wrote them immediately." She played with the sash on the new dress her fiancé had bought for her. "Gil is ready to pack up and follow me if it comes to that."

"That Gil is a keeper." Gemma smiled fondly, the happiness in her eyes was one of a true friend. "This is going to work out all right for you. I just know it, you wait and see. Now, what can I help you with?"

"We need more coffee." Maebry hated the money situation Maureen had left them in, so she hesitated in heading for the first aisle. "I know the ranch's account is past due. How much credit are you willing to give us?"

"Enough to keep you and those cowboys in coffee." With a shrug, Gemma headed in the opposite direction. "It will work out with Nate handling the estate. *Oh, no.* Duck and hide while you can."

"Why? What's wrong?" Maebry peered up the aisle, her stomach dropping at the sight of Gemma looking like a deer staring at the business end of a hunting rifle. Only one man could bring on that panicked look.

The bell above the door chimed like a musical death knell. A man entered the door and swept off his bowler, his gaze arrowing straight to Gemma. "Why, don't you look beautiful today, my lady? Like a breath of spring."

"Lawrence. Welcome to my family's store." Like a soldier ready to dash into enemy fire, Gemma straightened her shoulders, lifted her chin a notch and marched forward, her petticoats snapping. "What do you need today?"

"I'm not quite happy with my usual kind of tea." Lawrence's tenor held a note of adoration as he splayed his hands on the front counter, settling in like a man intending to stay awhile. "Perhaps you could suggest something new?"

Poor Gemma, Maebry thought as she peered between the shelves. At least she was safe from him now that she was officially off the market, thanks to Gil. She studied the section of coffee beans, debating. She'd better bake him some more cookies in gratitude.

The bell above the entrance chimed again. This time, little tingles shivered down Maebry's neck. Her heart opened the way a rose in springtime did, always blooming, always maturing. She peered between the shelves again, eager to drink in the sight of the big, strong cowboy moseying his way toward her with the confident strike of his boots.

Spotting her, he winked, his grin dominating his face, carving pleasant little crinkles around his adoring eyes.

"Gil." She breathed his name, felt the impact of it in her soul. "What are you doing here?"

"Got a note from Nate to drop by his office and see him." Gil strolled around the end of the aisle. Oh, he looked good. Tanned from the sun, rugged from the demanding work on the ranch, relaxed, as if he didn't have a single worry. "I have good news."

"Good news?" She nearly dropped the ten pound burlap sack of coffee beans she'd reached for. Luckily Gil leaned in, stole it from her and grabbed her free hand. "He heard from Maureen's heirs."

"The granddaughters." Maebry nearly stumbled. She'd gone numb all over, weak in the knees. "The McPhee sisters."

"Yes, they sent a telegram. Very thoughtful of them, considering." He held up the bag of coffee beans to Gemma so she could tally it in her book and opened the door.

She stepped through it, the blood in her veins jumping all over the place. So anxious, her feet didn't seem to be working properly. Somehow she stumbled onto the boardwalk, into the sweet caress of warm sunshine and the fresh, temperate breeze.

"They want me to move to Chicago, don't they? It won't be so bad. Really." She blew out a breath, wished she didn't feel lightheaded. Maybe she'd like Chicago. She was glad for Gil's towering presence beside her.

He didn't answer. That couldn't be a good sign. Instead, he ambled over to the railing, pitched the coffee bag gently into the back of the waiting wagon (yes, it had been freed from the mud mire by some of the ranch hands). Phil switched his tail, gave an annoyed nicker at being ignored, because Gil turned away from him, reaching for Maebry, holding her hands gently in his own.

Joy flickered in his bright blue eyes. His grin widened, dimples bracketed his mouth. "There will be no Chicago. You get to stay right here."

"In Bluebell?" She blinked, disbelieving, shaking her head, wanting to jump up and down. "Really? Are they coming here to the ranch?"

"I don't know, that wasn't mentioned. Just your contract. I have more good news." The rumble of Gil's laughter said everything. Bright, jubilant, full of bliss. "Nate wrote to them about you, of course, and suggested that they forgive the debt. They agreed to it, Maebry."

"They *what?*" Surely she hadn't heard him right. Who wouldn't want a free servant to cook and clean for them? She shook her head, saw that he was still grinning, that she hadn't imagined it. "You're not teasing me, are you? You mean that they've let me go, that I'm f-free?"

Even saying the word felt like a release. Gil was nodding, his happiness told her it was true, it was just so hard to process. Her life was really her own? Joy burst through her, a state of rapturous happiness that she'd never known before.

"It's really over." What glorious, wonderful words. "I can't believe it. I mean, I can do anything I want. I could work anywhere, do anything."

"Like marry me." Laughing, Gil pulled her into his arms, folding her against his hard chest. "I know you had your heart set on a long engagement, but considering this new turn of events, we could shorten it up a bit. Maybe get married in a couple of months."

"Months?" She tilted her head back, grinned up at him, so happy she was laughing too. She just couldn't stop. Just like she couldn't stop teasing him. "Oh, I don't know. That seems awfully fast. Don't rush me, Gil."

"I know how you feel," he joked, planting a kiss on her forehead. "I'm not the kind of man you can tie down, I like to roam, but considering this opportunity, maybe I can make the sacrifice."

"Gee, then maybe I could be talked into it, too." She was laughing when he kissed her left cheek, then her right, then he dropped a sweet kiss on her nose. "I'm thinking August will give me enough time to make a wedding dress."

"Good. Then tie me down in August." He cradled her chin in his hand, peered down lovingly into her eyes. When their gazes met, it was like their souls touched. He smiled. "Tie me down forever."

"I like the sound of that." She went up on tiptoe and brushed her lips across his. The sun chose that moment to brighten, spilling over them like a promise of happiness to come. A wonderful wedding, a happy marriage, a life lived together laughing all the way. Forever was right now, this very moment. She closed her eyes, gave in to his kiss, and let herself dream.

-The End-

The McPhee Clan continues in
MONTANA HEARTS
Daisy's story:

Rain sluiced down Daisy's cheeks and stung her eyes as she spotted two faint lights hovering in the darkness behind her. The wind whipped against her, and she felt every mile of the wide open plains. There were no lights from a nearby house, no one to hear her scream for help. As a city girl from the streets of Chicago, she felt out of her element, vulnerable and too isolated as the lights became closer. She could see the lanterns on the support posts of the covered buckboard.

Maybe whoever that was holding the reins of that horse coming their way could be an outlaw or a bandit or worse. Her heart dropped as the horses plodded to a stop.

"Hi there, Miss." A deep voice spoke from the shadows of the vehicle. "Looks like you've got a problem."

"Just a broken axle."

"I'd say that's a problem." The springs of the buckboard squeaked slightly and a shadow emerged. A big shadow. Mile-wide shoulders. Powerful masculine strength. He towered a good foot above her. The lantern light reflected on the gun holstered to his hip and thigh. A big handgun.

She gulped. Definitely an outlaw. Her blood turned to ice. "We don't have anything of value."

"Don't be afraid. I'm not here to rob you. I'm here to help." His stride was easy, not predatory, and the darkness favored him, as if doing its best to keep the lantern light from finding him. She heard more than saw him kneel down to look at the axle.

"Sorry to tell you this is no easy fix." He rose and his boots splashed in the mud in front of her. His presence blocked the stinging rain. "You must be Maureen's granddaughter."

"How did you know?"

"Five women traveling alone in these parts is one clue. Five city women. With folks in town gossiping the way they are, it's an easy guess." His voice turned to warmed molasses, rich and deep and inviting. "Maureen is long since buried."

"You knew my grandmother?" She slid a little in the mud as she crept closer.

"Very well." He shook his head in a sorry way, as if he couldn't believe what he was seeing. "Didn't the attorney tell you in his instructions to hire a driver?"

"I saw no need for the expenditure." Her chin shot up. She'd never seen a more masculine specimen. His broad chest, rock-solid arms and chiseled face looked carved from granite. Lightning blazed, thunder boomed and darkness fell in quick succession, leaving his image emblazoned upon her eyelids. "This may be my first time driving a team, but I've done perfectly fine."

"I can't believe you'd risk these roads in a storm. Glad I came across you when I did."

"Me, too." There was something about the man that tied her stomach in a knot. He was a stranger, and just because he'd known their grandmother didn't mean he was a good man. Or a safe man, she thought with a shiver. "Just who are you?"

"The name's Kincaid. Beckett Kincaid." His molasses-dark voice rumbled over her. She tingled in the strangest way, like she'd been too close to lightning.

ABOUT THE AUTHOR

Jillian Hart makes her home in Washington State, where she has lived most of her life. When Jillian is not writing away on her next book, she can be found reading, going to lunch with friends and spending quiet evenings at home with her family.

Made in the USA
San Bernardino, CA
06 January 2014